pizza my heart

pizza
my
heart

Rhiannon Richardson

SCHOLASTIC INC.

Copyright © 2022 by Rhiannon Richardson

Photos © Shutterstock.com

All rights reserved. Published by Scholastic Inc., *Publishers since 1920*. SCHOLASTIC and associated logos are trademarks and/or registered trademarks of Scholastic Inc.

ISBN 978-1-338-78438-1

10 9 8 7 6 5 4 3 2 1   22 23 24 25 26

Printed in the U.S.A.   40

First printing 2022

Book design by Yaffa Jaskoll

For all the friends who made my spontaneous
move to Ohio the wild, challenging, fun,
and memorable experience that it was.

chapter 1

"I can't believe you're abandoning me," my best friend, Sasha, whines, looping her arm through mine as we cross the street.

Abandoning is hardly the right word. That would imply that I'm going willingly when, really, I'm being dragged kicking and screaming into this new version of my life.

"I'm being kidnapped," I correct her.

Sasha laughs and shakes her head, her strawberry-scented cocoa-brown curls bouncing. The *thwack* of our flip-flops is rhythmic, thumping almost on beat with the basketball game in full swing at the park across the street. Some of the guys in our neighborhood get together on Friday evenings to play. My dad joins in sometimes, when he's not working. Since Fridays are one of the busier nights at Soul Slice, *sometimes* means *almost never*.

But now that we're moving, I guess there won't even be *sometimes* anymore.

At the beginning of summer, moving day felt eons away. Suddenly it's almost here, a presence so distinct it might as well loop its arm through my free one and walk with Sasha and me.

Starting tomorrow, there will be no more running down to the corner store anytime I've got a craving for Takis or hot fries, demolishing the bag as I head to Sasha's brownstone, asking her mom to let me in so I can wash Taki dust off my red-tinted fingertips before Sasha and I plot our next adventure.

No more subway rides to Manhattan, to roam around the bookstore that's four stories tall, stop at the café that serves the best croissants, and buy art supplies (me) and makeup (Sasha). No more Washington Square Park, lunches by the arch, or weaving our way up to the Garment District so I can pick out fabric for my mom to sew into shirts.

I was born and raised here in Brooklyn, and I love New York. I love how there's always a new cobblestone street to explore, always a new boutique or museum. But now, no more city. And no more Sasha.

"Hey," Sasha says, pulling me from my well of nostalgia. "Look at it like a fresh start."

"I don't want a fresh start," I remind her, though she's not the one I need to make my case to.

My parents never said, *Hey, Maya, what do you think about picking up and moving to the outskirts of Philadelphia to open a second pizza shop?* I give them a little credit because obviously I would've said, *Hard pass.* Still, I used to be under the impression that where *I* lived had a little something to do with *me*. Now I know it has nothing to do with how I feel or what I want. It's all about my parents and their dreams. Speaking of which . . .

Sasha and I turn the corner and approach my parents' pizza place. Soul Slice is wedged between a dry cleaner's and the aforementioned Takis-selling corner store. It's a hole-in-the-wall, distinguished by the SOUL SLICE block lettering above the door, the green paint faded from age. Through the front window, I see Mom behind the counter ringing up customers, and Dad in the back by the pizza oven.

"So, this is where the road ends," I say, dragging out my words in a sigh. "Are you sure you can't smuggle me into your basement for a few weeks until my parents give up on looking for me?" I ask Sasha, only half kidding.

Sasha gasps, play-slapping my arm. "Maya, *stop*."

I can't help but laugh, imagining myself hiding amid all the random things Sasha's family exiles to the basement. I could probably fit inside one of the ridiculously giant ceramic vases her grandma sends every Christmas.

"I had to at least try," I say, shrugging. "But, for real," I add, "I love you."

Sasha looks at me, her bushy eyebrows pinched in the middle of her forehead.

"I love you, too." She pouts, which makes me pout.

Sasha's phone vibrates, and I know it's her mom asking where she is. I guilted her into hanging out a little while longer, but now there's no more overtime.

We head into Soul Slice, immediately enveloped in the humid, pizza-scented air. I've basically grown up in this shop, with its sand-colored walls and matching linoleum tile floor. The air conditioner hasn't worked right in years, so we keep the door cracked open, which helps to draw in customers. You can smell the basil, oregano, fresh tomatoes, and melted cheese from blocks away. There are also the delicious scents of syrup, corn bread, fried chicken, and gravy from our specialty pizzas.

I squeeze behind the counter, saying hi to Thomas and Renee, who have worked here longer than I can remember. They're going to stay in New York and run the shop while we open Soul Slice 2.0.

Lucky them.

I sign in to the closed register so I can ring up Sasha's order. Even though I'm not technically an employee, I have an employee ID number that I use to sign in whenever my parents need me to cover the registers while one of them is on break or in the back for a meeting.

Sasha orders her usual—a Corn Bread Crust pie

that she'll bring home to her family for dinner. While her pizza's getting prepared, Sasha goes to say her goodbyes to my parents, who each give her a hug. When Sasha's pizza is ready, I hand her the warm cardboard box and then walk with her to the door.

"See you later, crocodile?" I say, like always.

"In a while, alligator," she says, her smile lopsided.

We hug each other, and I inhale the familiar strawberry smell of my best friend's hair. Then I watch from the window as she heads up the block. She turns around to wave to me before disappearing around the corner.

"Maya, honey," Mom says, appearing beside me. She wipes her hands on her apron. "Did you have a good day with Sasha?"

"Yeah," I say, because it's true, no matter how much it hurts that it was our *last* day.

"Dad and I are about to finish up here," Mom says, reaching for the end of one of my French braids, twirling it around her finger. "Why don't you hang out for a minute and then we can all walk home together and finish packing?"

Though it sounds like a question, I know I don't have a choice. While Mom retreats to the back of the store to get Dad, I slide into one of the empty booths.

It's been about two months since my parents broke the news to me about the move. "It'll be a new chapter in our story" is how Mom put it.

"We'll open the store, start expanding," Dad had said.

"And what, we move every time you want to open a store?" I'd asked, stunned. "We plant roots only for you to rip them up again?"

My parents had stared at me, clearly not expecting me to be so against this life-changing decision they made *without* me.

"Well, no," Dad had said after a beat.

"So, if we don't have to move for every store opening, then why do we have to move for this one?" I was quick. My grandma told me that once, and right then I felt like I was channeling my smart-mouth quickness powers, as if they'd actually do something.

"This is our first expansion, that's why. If this goes smoothly, then we shouldn't have to be there for every one after it," Mom explained, only there was an edge in her voice.

She doesn't like when I push. They never like when I push. And I've never had a reason to, not really, before now.

I reach into my shorts pocket and take out my phone. I remember how excited I was back in May when my parents got me a new phone for my birthday. Come to find out, it was supposed to soften the blow.

"You'll be able to call and text Sasha whenever you want. And FaceTime," Mom had reasoned.

Turning it over in my hands now, a selfie of Sasha and me smiling up at me from my lock screen, I can admit that the phone is nice and I'm grateful for it. However, I really don't want to FaceTime my best friend only to get some pixelated version of her face. And texting isn't the same as talking in person. I can't hype up a nugget of gossip, or relay how suspect someone is, or express my *Oh no no NO* when something's got me worked up.

I gaze around Soul Slice. The pictures on the wall are blown-up photographs of Italy—where my mom's mom lived before she came to America—and of our family.

When my parents first opened their pizza shop, it was called Reynolds' Pizza, after our family name. We weren't really a popular spot. But one day, a customer told my dad how much he loved that he and my mom could combine their respective culinary backgrounds into their signature slices. When I asked if he meant soul food and pizza, the metaphoric ship was christened and set to sail.

Soul Slice is the culinary child of my mom's Italian heritage and my dad's Southern roots. My parents claimed their brand and told the world what made them special. As a result, our small pizza shop turned into a *thing*. Now that *thing* has grown into a beast that's forcing me out of Brooklyn and into the suburbs of freaking Philadelphia.

Suburb to me means unseasoned meat, inauthentic ethnic food made in white-owned restaurants, more land than there are things to do, and a lot of golden retrievers. No Brooklyn Bridge, no East River, and no delightfully dizzying maze of high-rise buildings.

I let out a breath. My brain has been a tornado of all the reasons why moving is the *worst* idea *ever*. But I know none of it matters and my being upset won't change anything. The sooner I accept it, the better ... or something like that.

The photo on the wall next to me is one my grandpa took before he passed away. I was a baby, giggling at the camera. My parents were smiling, excited to have me. I was the perfect combination of Dad's dark apple cheeks and Mom's soft curly hair. My dad used to say that they would move heaven and earth if it meant they could put a smile on my face.

Yet now they're moving all of *us* ... for some pizza.

chapter 2

In my new bedroom in Hempstead, Pennsylvania, I finally finish folding my clothes and shut my dresser drawers. Next, I move on to the box labeled SHOES. I'm relieved to find that my shoes aren't a complete mess. My clothes got wrinkled on the ride over in the moving truck this morning. Shoes, however—bless their little paired-up souls—can't *unfold*. I put the shoes away in record time in my walk-in closet and decide that—if I have to pick a positive about all this—I can appreciate that our house is bigger, which means my room is bigger, too. We also have a yard now.

But I would happily sacrifice having my own yard to go to Prospect Park with Sasha so that we can hang out in the shade of the trees, or visit the Grand Army

Plaza fountain on particularly hot days, letting the mist cool us. Driving from Brooklyn to Hempstead to the new house, I haven't seen *one* fountain or *one* amazing park. Just sayin'.

I start flattening some of the empty boxes to make more space in my room. I have my twin bed pushed up against one wall with my nightstand beside it, just like in my old room.

"Looks like everything is coming together," Dad says from my doorway, surprising me.

"Oh my gosh!" I suck in a breath, laughing a little.

"Didn't mean to startle you, kid," he says, his smile so wide his eyes squint. "Your room is almost all set up . . . exactly how it used to be?"

"That's the plan," I say, hoping I sound as stubborn as I am.

Dad raises his eyebrows and does one more scan of my room, mentally assessing the number of boxes I have left. It's the same scan he does when he takes inventory at the shop.

"Where's the party?" Mom asks from the hallway.

She comes up behind Dad and rests her chin on his shoulder, flashing me an equally large smile. "WOW, honey, look how much you got done."

"I honestly just want to get this over with," I say, hoping they don't try to make a big deal out of everything.

"Well, you're gonna have to take a break," she says. "It's time for us to head over to see our new shop and finally meet our employees in person."

I want to remind her that *I* don't have a new shop and that *I* didn't go hiring a bunch of people based on their Zoom call etiquette. But then I would get in trouble for being fresh. So instead, I step out of my room, sending up a little prayer that this visit to the pizza place doesn't take forever.

∘♥∘♥∘

Soul Slice 2.0 sits between a ballet studio and a hardware store. Seeing as I have next to no rhythm, the last thing I care about is a dance studio. I do, however, love the smell of paint and sawdust. I love arts and crafts and building things. But there's no time to pop into the hardware store. Dad holds open the Soul Slice door, and Mom and I file inside.

I gasp. Soul Slice 2.0 is an eyesore. The floor is concrete, and the walls are bare. The ceiling is almost finished, but there are still wires dangling, waiting to be connected to . . . something. Currently, the only saving grace is that the room actually *feels* air-conditioned.

The place is a blank slate, and I guess my parents can turn it into anything they want.

I'd be lying if I said this wasn't a little bit exciting.

"What do you think?" Dad asks, his voice echoing.

I look at my parents, standing next to each other, backlit from the sunshine flooding through the windows. I wonder if this is how they looked when they first opened Reynolds' Pizza—angelic, eager, and younger somehow.

"The more important question is 'What do *you* think?'" I say, deflecting because there's no way I can let them know I might actually come to like Soul Slice 2.0.

Dad takes a deep breath, his boxy shoulders rising up to his ears and promptly dropping again. Mom runs her hands through her short curly hair.

"There's a lot of work to be done," she admits. "We

have an interior designer coming this week. We'll figure out colors, furniture, decor, and hopefully by the end of the month, we can have our grand opening."

"I thought we're opening tomorrow," I say, confused.

"We'll be open for *deliveries*," Mom explains. "The kitchen is finished, so we can start making pizzas immediately. But once we can actually have customers inside, it would be nice to announce it to the community and officially welcome everyone with a party."

A knock at the window makes us jump. I see a few people standing outside the shop—they must be the new Soul Slice employees. Dad waves them in, and they join us inside.

"Welcome, welcome," Dad greets them, his voice booming.

"So nice to meet you. Thank you for coming," Mom says.

"I'm Maya," I say, reminding myself to smile.

"Jean," the first guy says. He has on a pair of baggy jeans and beat-up blue New Balances. His hair reminds me of Shaggy from *Scooby-Doo*, which seems incredibly fitting.

"I'm Denise," says a Black girl with Bantu knots. She smiles and reaches out a hand with long blue ombré acrylic nails. Her skin is warm, and I catch faint scents of vanilla and cinnamon, probably from her lotion. Looking at our hands intertwined, I see that her skin nearly matches the chestnut color of mine. "I see you, with the fit. Cute, girl," she adds.

I hadn't given much thought to my outfit before now. I'm wearing denim shorts and one of the shirts Mom made for me from batik fabric. Batiks are hand-dyed fabrics with designs set in from laid wax. I love the bright colors and patterns. Thankfully Mom loves to sew, so my wardrobe always stays fresh, which I'm grateful for right now. Currently, I have on a lime-green top with pale green fish dyed into it.

"Thanks," I say, my smile no longer forced.

"I'm Trevor," the next guy greets us, shaking my hand enthusiastically and smiling before looking back at my parents to say, "Wow, she looks just like y'all."

"Well, I am their daughter," I say quietly, laughing a little awkwardly.

Next, I meet Chris, Jamie, and Farrah, and once we

are all introduced, Mom gets right down to business with an official tour.

We walk from the customer territory at the front of the shop back to employee territory. There's the delivery station, which has a counter, a register, two convection ovens to keep finished pizzas warm, and shelves filled with boxes. Beyond that is the kitchen, with its industrial sink for washing dishes, and a shimmering reflective stainless-steel oven. Next to the oven is the topping line, where pizzas are assembled. The dough is preset in pans that will be stacked up in the annex where Dad will make the dough. He'll then store the extra dough in the fridge, where we also keep all the toppings and cheese.

Next to the kitchen is the office, where Mom can shut herself away to do administrative work and dictate the fate of her pizza kingdom.

"Any questions?" Mom asks when the tour is complete.

Dad raises his hand, and Mom calls on him.

"Did it hurt when you fell from heaven?" he asks, making everyone laugh.

Something stiff inside me cracks up with everyone

else. I can't remember the last time I saw my mom blush. Even though she's tired, she looks beautiful and in her element. I feel a rush of pride.

"Any *pizza-related* questions?" she asks, regaining her composure.

When no one else raises their hand, she goes on to assign the stations. "Trevor and Jean will run the topping line. Chris and Farrah, you'll handle phones. Jamie, you'll be our designated dishwasher and restocker. And Denise and Maya, you'll run deliveries. Now, I'm still—"

"Wait, what?" I blurt.

Everyone turns to look at me.

"Yes, Maya?" Mom says, holding her notepad against her chest.

"Did you say *I'm* doing deliveries?" I ask, hoping I misheard her.

"Yes."

Right. No explanation. No warning. Sounds familiar.

I hold myself together for the rest of my parents' orientation, waiting for the other employees to leave.

Once Dad locks the door behind Trevor and Jamie, I speak up.

"Mom, I don't want to be a delivery driver. Plus, it's pretty hard to be a *driver* when I *can't drive*."

"You have the bike we got you for your birthday," Mom reminds me.

I guess this means the bike was another fake gift meant to make the move "easier."

"Are you being serious?" I ask, leaning against the counter.

Mom sighs. "I'm sorry, Maya, but we need your help. For now, at least, while we get things up and running."

"And look," Dad adds, "it won't be forever, and you'll get to keep tips on top of your allowance. How about that?"

"Plus, you'll get the lay of the land, riding your bike all over Hempstead. Soon, you'll be showing *us* around," Mom says, trying to sound positive.

I'm not convinced. Being the new girl in town *and* the pizza delivery person sounds like a recipe for disaster.

chapter 3

The next day, I'm standing in Soul Slice 2.0, sweating in my OG Soul Slice army-green employee T-shirt. The seven-hundred-degree oven is pumping out more pizzas than I thought possible for a store that's not even technically OPEN. Still, word must have gotten out because we're getting lots of calls for deliveries.

Not that I've made one yet. As the only delivery *driver*, Denise handles all the orders—and tips, I might add—for houses outside a certain block-radius of the shop.

"It's so hot, I feel like I'm going to pass out," I tell Mom, peeking into her office. So much for a working air conditioner.

"Maybe you need some air." Mom sighs, chucking her pen into the holder at the edge of her desk.

"Air, as in *outside*?" I ask, trying not to get my hopes up at the possibility of being able to leave and put this whole "delivery" nonsense behind me . . . at least for today.

"Yes," she says, a smile taking over her face.

I follow Mom out into the main area of the shop. Looking at the glass door, I see freedom calling my name in the form of sunshine and a dying summer day. Dusk is when the temperature goes down and the sky turns pink, and last night revealed that there are even more fireflies out here in the suburbs than in the city—another possible positive about the move.

"Maya, hey," Mom says behind me.

I stop and turn. Mom is in front of the delivery register, one hand on her hip and the other on her mouth, stifling a laugh.

"Hey?" I head toward her.

Mom gestures to the orders flashing on the register screen. "These next couple orders are close enough to bike to. How about you take them and see how it feels?"

The promise of being outside gives me some hope. I help Mom put two boxes inside an insulated delivery bag that will keep the pizzas hot. She follows me out the front door, where, surprisingly, we find Dad kneeling by my bike. His bald head glistens under the golden-hour sunshine with beads of sweat.

This morning, he attached a basket above my back wheel for the boxes to sit in. Now he's twisting the wrench fast, attaching some contraption to my handlebars.

"Hey, sweetie," he says without looking up. He twists the wrench until the bolt is locked in. "This should hold up well."

Hopefully not too well, I think, figuring the only way I might get out of making these deliveries is if my bike falls apart.

"It's starting to get dark," Mom says, more to Dad than to me.

Dad nods. "I think after these deliveries it'll be safe for you to call it a day."

"Don't play with me," I say, a smile blooming inside. It's one thing if Mom says the day *might* be over soon, but those words mean something completely different when Dad says it.

"We really appreciate you helping out, Maya," he adds, using the hem of his T-shirt to wipe the sweat from his brow. "But we don't want you out too late the night before your first day of school."

Right. My first day of seventh grade, starting over at a new school with no friends. I almost forgot about that.

My parents help me secure the delivery bag to the back of my bike, and Dad walks me through the phone attachment on my handlebars that he installed so I can use the GPS. It's becoming harder to believe that my helping out was not some incredibly premeditated plan. Nevertheless, I wave to my parents before pushing off, following the blue trail on my phone.

Usually, the summer air is a nice feeling, the way the sunshine kisses my skin. But after spending most of the day circling an oven hotter than the desert, the outside heat merely annoys me. As I ride, I can feel my hair getting slimy under my Soul Slice cap. My braids stick to the back of my neck, and I realize what I want more than anything is to take a long, cold shower.

I cruise by the small strip of shops known as downtown Hempstead and follow my GPS through a neighborhood a few streets over from mine. I've noticed that a lot of families around here have dogs. A couple of dogs hover outside on the porches, and others play fetch in the yard with their families, taking breaks to roll around in the grass. Most of the lawns are mowed, the smell of cut grass new and refreshing. Most of the "lawns" in Brooklyn are concrete slabs barely big enough for a patio table and small charcoal grill.

I come to a stop in front of the first house, get off my bike, and ring the bell with the pizza box in hand.

"Are you the daughter of the Soul Slice owners? That's so industrious," Mrs. McIntyre, the first customer, tells me. I wait for her to hand me the money before I trade the pizza with her. "I wish my daughter showed some interest in her father's business."

I hold back from telling her not to wish that on her kid, since it's not my place by a long shot.

"I just try to help out," I say instead.

Mrs. McIntyre considers me for a moment, a smile spreading across her red-tinted lips. "Here, why don't you take this and keep it for yourself," she says all *hush-hush*. She holds out an extra five dollars to me, and I happily accept it.

"Thank you."

Making a little money of my own *could* be an upside to doing deliveries. I shove the five in my back-right pocket and keep the shop money and change purse in my front left one, not wanting to risk mixing the two. I head back to my bike, typing in the address that—thank goodness—marks my last task for today.

This delivery takes me into a cul-de-sac with a NO OUTLET sign. The houses here are huge, the lawns perfectly manicured. The walkways are lined with fresh stinky mulch and flower bushes boasting of their brightness.

I roll to a stop in front of a tall and wide dark brown house with black trim on the windows and roof. The house is set back, the walkway dipping down a few steps before reaching the front door. A stainless-steel mosquito lamp hisses. I don't know if it's the setting sun or the towering demeanor of the house, but something about it seems unwelcoming.

Still, a delivery is a delivery, no matter where it takes me.

I head down the walkway, hopping off the last step onto the porch, feeling hopeful since, on the other side of this exchange, my freedom is waiting. I tap the doorbell and an elaborate chime unfolds behind the door. It's like something from a movie about rich people, which—I guess—makes it fitting. Through the frosted glass panel next to the door, I see a figure coming toward me. I stand up straighter, double-checking the receipt to see that someone named Justin placed the order.

"You're late," a kid says, the door not even all-the-way open.

"Well, hello," I say, looking past him to see if his mom or dad is coming.

"Hello?" he says, waving at me.

Oh no he didn't. Rude.

"It's thirteen seventy-five," I tell him, not wanting to prolong this by even a second.

The kid shakes his head, his brown eyes frosting over with something mean.

"You're late. Isn't there some kind of rule that the pizza is free if the delivery is late?"

"Not with Soul Slice."

He rolls his eyes before looking down to pull some cash out of the front pocket of his black khakis. Only uppity kids wear khakis instead of jeans. With his head bent, I notice the waves in his fade, the dark brown ripples glossy and nearly perfect. When he looks back up, a smirk stretched across his mouth, I notice a mole above his lip.

He hands me a twenty, so I hand him the pizza and start counting change. Low-key, I wait for him to say to keep the extra as tip, but that never comes.

Instead, he says, "I want my money back. This is all wrong."

"What do you mean, it's *all wrong*?" I ask, just about ready to snatch the pizza and leave.

"I didn't ask for peppers, I asked for *capers*, and I

hate black olives. I asked for green. And pepperoni is pork; I don't eat pork. I asked for *pepperoncini*. I can't eat this."

I sigh, resisting the urge to give him a piece of my mind. Instead, I hand him back the twenty and simultaneously grab the pizza box from him.

"Where are you going?" he asks when I turn on my heel.

"Um, that's none of your business."

"What are you doing with my pizza?"

I turn back around and stare at him. He's standing there, in his uppity black khakis, a white T-shirt, and—oh, how did I miss this?—a gold chain around his neck. A wannabe G.

"What is it, then? Your pizza? Or an inedible disaster?" I ask.

"I want to talk to your manager."

I gesture all around us, to my empty bike, the empty porch, the front yard. "Go. Right. Ahead."

"Seriously? You're the worst."

"Why?" I demand, my anger growing. "Because I rode my bike here as fast as I could to deliver you a still-hot pizza that was, what"—I stop and check the receipt to find that the pizza was—oh *yes*—"three minutes late! THREE MINUTES!"

"Don't forget that it's an ineducable disaster," he adds.

"And inedu-what? Can you speak English?"

"I'm going to give you a bad review," he threatens.

"You don't even know who I am!"

"Well, I know you work at Soul Slice," he snaps.

"Yeah, and so do my parents. Call them up, tell them how you were too good for this perfectly fine pizza and treated me like dirt," I hiss, snatching up the last word and heading out of there before I can say anything worse than I already have.

I don't see the first step on the walkway, and I trip.

I pitch forward, the pizza box flies open, and I fall onto a thin cushion of oily cheese, pepperoni, olives, and red sauce. Unfortunately, the cardboard top doesn't soften the blow of my chin hitting the ground. *Ouch.* I grit my teeth, picking myself up to find my knees scraped and my uniform covered in pizza.

I try to take a deep breath, but it wobbles inside

me, tears stinging my eyes. I'm not hurt so much as I'm embarrassed. In the interest of not having this brat laugh at me and call my parents to complain about me littering on his front walkway, I gather up the soiled box and run to my bike, not looking back.

"Wait, are you okay? *Wait!*" the boy calls after me.

"Just leave me alone!" I shout.

I push off from the curb, using the back of my hand to keep my tears from blurring my vision, and pedal away as fast as I can.

chapter 4

Instead of telling my parents the truth, I throw the wrecked pizza in a dumpster and use falling off my bike as an explanation for the scrapes and bruises. Mom, worried, immediately drives me home and finishes sewing the shirt she's been making me. She also gives me box braids as a thank-you for being a "good sport" about everything.

So, aside from the scrapes on my knee and the Band-Aid I have front and center on my chin, at least I can start seventh grade with some good hair and a bomb new batik tee. This one is dark green with pastel-orange sunflowers. And the box braids trail down my back, golden yarn woven into a few for a nice accent. The coconut oil gives them a shine, and every once in a while, I can catch the oil fragrance on the gentle breeze blowing past me as I ride my bike to school the next morning.

Don't get me wrong, I'm still *not* excited. Not only am I starting seventh grade without Sasha by my side, but lucky me has to help out at Soul Slice 2.0 this afternoon.

Hempstead Middle School is a short boxy building. I find the bike rack easily enough, but the rest of the campus is like a maze. A month ago, I got a virtual tour of the school online and filled out a few forms and questionnaires. The school emailed my parents a list of supplies and a map, which I forgot to print out after being consumed with yesterday's disaster. So, I have notebooks and pens in my backpack but no idea where I'm going.

I follow the droves of students into what I assume is the main entrance and up a tall staircase. At the top, I notice a kid out of breath and am thankful that I'm so used to walking everywhere. Another thing I'm thankful for is the sign reading MAIN OFFICE dead in front of me.

Once I tell the receptionist my name, she has me take a seat while she prints a copy of my schedule and a school map. I take a moment to check my phone. I texted Sasha *Happy First Day* with a crocodile emoji, and she responded with a thumbs-up and a heart. I miss her already.

"Oh my gosh!" a green-haired girl with olive skin and a fresh pair of Birkenstocks squeals from the office entryway. "I love your hair," she says. "And OMG, that *shirt*."

"Thank you, I like yours, too—your hair, I mean," I say, sitting up a little when she plops down into the seat next to me. Maybe this is a sign. I was worried I might be the only new kid, and now this green-haired savior has floated into my life. "I'm Maya."

"I'm Devin," she says. She holds out a hand with white-and-green polka-dot nails, which I promptly shake. "You have no idea how awesome it is to finally have someone new here."

"You're not new?" I ask, trying not to deflate.

She scrunches her brows together, confused. "I'm your buddy."

My turn to be confused. "My buddy?" I ask.

"Yeah, like, the person who shows you around. The Michael to your Cameron James, the Cher Horowitz to your Tai Frasier."

"*10 Things I Hate About You* and *Clueless*?" I confirm.

"OMG, so you have awesome hair, sick style, *and* excellent movie taste," Devin says.

"They're classics," I admit, but quickly backtrack. "Hold on, though. You're my *buddy*?"

"Didn't you take a survey at your new student orientation?"

"Yes." There was one called an Interests Survey that I remember feeling flattered but confused about because schools don't usually care about students' specific interests.

"So, the survey helps the school 'get to know the students,'" she says, using air quotes. "They say they tailor the events and organize clubs based on mass interest, but I don't buy it. However, the one thing the surveys are good for is pairing new kids up with students who have shared interests . . . It would make more sense if we actually had new students *regularly*, but hey, here we are now."

"So, you're saying we have shared interests?"

Before she can answer, Mrs. Abner comes back with my schedule and map. Even with the map in hand, I'm glad to have Devin glued to my side so that I'm not wading through the ocean of students by myself—especially since I have that Band-Aid on my face. I reach up to touch it as we weave through the crowd of laughing, talking kids.

"We have shared interests," Devin confirms, leading me past the library. "Such as art. I'll show you the art department."

Art! I can't help but feel excited. Even though Sasha supports my artistic pursuits, she herself does not like to wield anything other than a debit card. For every magazine she buys, I'll buy a sketchbook. For every brow pencil, I'd find a charcoal one. For every TikTok dance routine she works on, I draw, paint, and sculpt something. We balance each other out, for sure. But I'd be lying if I said I never once wished we could paint something together or brainstorm sculpture ideas.

Devin leads me down a stairwell. When we emerge in the downstairs hallway, I realize I'm taking my first breath that doesn't smell of Axe body spray and bleach. This fairly empty hallway smells like paint and wood.

We pass a mural of Mother Teresa made of old CD covers, and a loom with a floor-to-ceiling woven rug hung on the wall next to it. The tribal patterns stand out with bold contrasting colors. Upon closer inspection, you can see the starts and stops of thread, where the weaver made knots before continuing. And each tassel at the end is tied off in a slightly different way. I've never seen anything like it, nor have I ever fathomed *making* something like it myself.

"This is awesome," I say, not even embarrassed to be geeking out. "My old school didn't have a big arts program, not like this," I add.

"Well, it's not *that* big," Devin says.

"Are all of these pieces student artwork?" I ask, spotting a sculpture of a tree with carved tree bark and little humans walking in and out of holes, like the trunk is a house.

"Yes, and this is one of the art rooms."

We walk into a classroom, leaving the decorated hallway behind. Inside, it's a cave of art supplies organized on shelves made from scrap wood. The walls are a collage of works in progress and finished projects. There are still-life sketches and portraits, landscape oil paintings, sculptures made from wires and leaves and clay and corks. It's heaven.

On the far side of the classroom, I spot a drawing table. A real, tilted drawing table. I've always wanted one. That way I could sketch and draw for hours without getting cramps in my back or feeling tired from slouching over.

"Please tell me I have an art class in this room," I tell Devin.

"Seventh graders can't take art," Devin says with a sigh.

"WHAT!" I say, a little louder than intended. But still, my outrage is totally warranted.

The Brooklyn schools might've been underfunded, leaving the art department to basically fend for itself, but *at least* I could take a class when I wanted.

"I know, I know. But—take a deep breath before

you explode," Devin instructs, smiling at my frantic expression. "There aren't enough art teachers to accommodate sixth, seventh, *and* eighth graders. So, art *classes* are reserved for eighth graders, but art *club* is open to everyone," she explains, amusement still sparkling in her eyes.

"Art club?" I say slowly, still cautious because I don't think I can stand having my hopes shattered once again.

"Yes, after school on Wednesdays," she says. "Anyone can be in art club, and if you're in art club, then you can enter the art festival that happens at the end of the month."

Before I can ask about the festival, a voice says, "Are you recruiting more people for our cult?"

Devin turns around as a girl comes into the classroom. She has purple streaks in her shoulder-length black hair. The contrast with her pale skin is striking, but in a pretty way.

"I'm Mikayla," she says, reaching out a hand.

"Maya," I say, shaking it.

"Mikayla is in art club, too," Devin says.

"So how does the festival work, exactly?" I ask them both.

"The festival is how we show donors why they should keep funding the art department," Mikayla explains.

"And it's an art competition," Devin adds. "We have artists from the community come in to judge. They vote based on categories like sculpture, drawing, painting, photography, and also things like originality and design. If you win first place, you get a ribbon."

"But you have to be in art club to participate," Mikayla adds. "Not sure if she mentioned that."

"Do I have to sign up for art club somewhere?" I ask, excited by the thought of my own art potentially winning a prize.

Devin picks up a nearby graphite pencil, puffs out her chest, and taps me on each shoulder. "I now ordain you an art club member," she says in a poor British accent.

Going along with it, I take a bow. "Why, thank you, Your Highness," I say, and we all crack up.

"Seriously, though," Mikayla adds, "you just have

to show up Wednesdays after school. Mr. Chris takes attendance for each meeting."

I nod. "I can do that." I can't wait.

After being a saint and showing me where my locker is, Devin has to head to her first-period class, and I have to go back to being brand-new.

I find my English class easily enough. The teacher— Mrs. Moore, according to my class schedule—even eliminated the anxiety of picking seats by assigning them. When I find my name placard, I sit down at my desk and feel some tension leave me.

Surveying the other names around me, I start with the placard on the desk across the aisle from me. It says JUSTIN BAKER.

Justin, as in the boy who ordered the pizza yesterday and was a huge jerk? I take a deep breath, reminding myself that Justin is a common name and I don't know that it's him for sure—

"Hey, it's you."

I look up and see the familiar uppity khakis and

that gold chain, glinting under the fluorescent lights. When we do lock eyes, recognition flashes for both of us. It's *him*.

"I'm sorry about your face," Justin says, his voice quiet.

Excuse me? I can't tell if it's an insult or he's actually apologizing for the fact that he caused me to need a bandage. It doesn't matter either way.

"Sorry about your existence," I hiss, keeping my voice low so the teacher won't hear.

At this, *his* face scrunches up. "*Hey.* I just wanted to say—"

"There's nothing you can say. Leave me alone."

He raises his eyebrows, gesturing to the name placard across from me.

Justin sits, but I stand, avoiding his questioning eyes as I go to the front of the room, where Mrs. Moore's desk is. She's hunched over a notebook, writing intently with her glasses halfway down her nose. I try to wait until she finishes, but when the first bell rings and more students start coming into the classroom, I decide I just want to get this over with.

"Excuse me, Mrs. Moore?"

She looks up through her bangs, somewhat startled. But the smile that quickly slips across her face makes me feel more confident about my request.

"Maya, right?" she asks, reaching for a paper underneath her notebook. "Maya Reynolds. Welcome," she adds, her voice light.

"Thank you. I—uh—am wondering if I might be allowed to switch seats. Justin and I don't really get along."

She glances over at Justin, who's sitting in his seat with his notebook open like a perfectly behaved student. Ugh.

"Well, that's impressive," Mrs. Moore says, surprising me.

I switch my attention back to her. "It is?"

"It's your first day, and you already don't get along with someone," she says, though her brow is quirked like it's a question. Before I can try to explain or at least speak in my defense, she adds, "Now, that's all the more reason for the two of you to work together, don't you think?"

The cheery smile has since left her face, and she's looking at me with her head tilted to the side—like I should've known better than to ask this.

"I guess . . ." I say, realizing that my luck for today might have officially run out.

"Good. Plus, seating arrangements are non-negotiable. If I let you switch, then everyone would want to switch. It's easier this way."

"Right. Sorry," I say, imploding a little inside.

I go back to my seat and slump down, reminding myself to cling to the positives and *ignore* the negatives.

"Maya," Justin whispers.

Ignore. Ignore. Ignore.

"I really am—" he starts saying, but the second bell rings, cutting him off.

I focus my attention on the front of the class, where Mrs. Moore stands and starts referencing the Smart Board. Unfortunately, Justin is directly in my natural line of sight, and I catch him looking over at me.

The end of first period can't come soon enough. I'm relieved when the bell rings, but before I can get up, Justin has the chance to slip me a piece of notebook paper. Without looking at him, I snatch the paper and leave. I feel like my head is spinning as I join the traffic of the hallway.

○ ♥ ○ ♥ ○

By the time Devin finds me at my locker before lunch, I'm amped up from reliving the memory of diving into Justin's pizza yesterday. I catch her up to speed on my drama as we sit down with Mikayla in the cafeteria.

"Sounds about right," Devin says, unzipping her lunch box. "Justin is one of the popular kids, and they're all pretty entitled."

"And now I'm stuck with him in English class for the whole year," I groan.

"Are you guys talking about Justin Baker?" Mikayla asks through a mouthful of macaroni and cheese.

Devin nods. "He was a total jerk to Maya yesterday. He managed to turn her bringing him a pizza into some kind of offense."

"*Seriously?* Next time, tell him to kick rocks and then bring the pizza to my house," Mikayla says.

"Gladly," I say, feeling a little better.

"Sighting at six o'clock," a red-haired girl says as she sits down across from Devin.

Devin and Mikayla turn to look at something, and I follow their eyes to see what the big deal is.

"What the . . . ?"

Emerging from the salad bar is Justin with a Devin look-alike. Well, she's basically what Devin would look like if Devin wasn't as original and outgoing with her hair and clothes. This girl is basic and toned down, with her nude eye shadow, straightened black hair, and denim miniskirt.

"Who is that?" I ask.

"That's my twin sister," Devin admits. "My *evil* twin."

"Her name is Waverly," the red-haired girl says before holding out a hand to me. "And I'm Sophie."

"Maya," I say, quickly wiping my hand on my napkin before shaking hers.

"I know. I mean, it's rare that we ever have anyone *new* here," Sophie admits, spearing her salad with her fork.

"So I've heard," I say, sharing a smile with Devin.

I watch as Justin and Waverly take their seats at a table by the windows.

"Are they dating?" I ask Devin, figuring it would make sense for a popular guy to date a popular girl.

Devin rolls her eyes. "No," she says. "But Waverly has a crush on him. He's all she talks about."

"Ugh," I say, but I'm a little intrigued. "What does she say?"

"According to my sister, Justin's favorite ice cream flavor is *choco choco chocolate*," Devin says, fake swooning. "And that he *loves*—loves, I tell you—his dog, Cher. And he's afraid of four-leaf clovers."

"What a unique bundle of information," I say. "And *Cher*?"

"Apparently his mom named the dog," Mikayla says with a smirk.

"I don't think Justin is as into Waverly as she's into him," Sophie observes, crunching on lettuce between every word.

"But they would be a match made in heaven," Devin admits, her smirk a little rueful. "A self-absorbed girl with a self-absorbed guy. They'd be too invested in themselves to ever have problems with each other."

"I'm sensing some tension there," I say to Devin.

At this, Sophie and Mikayla crack up.

"That's the understatement of the century," Mikayla says, giggling.

"Waverly and Devin hate each other. Tension would imply some *underlying* feelings, but they wear theirs on their sleeves," Sophie explains.

"Just a healthy sister rivalry," Devin says in a fake high-pitched voice that has me cracking up, too.

"For real, though," Sophie cuts in. "Back to the important things. Why is the owner of a pizza shop eating a turkey sub for lunch?"

All eyes turn to me and the sandwich I packed this morning.

"First, I'm not an *owner*. I'm the owners' daughter. Second, what—am I supposed to eat pizza every day?" I ask, feeling a little self-conscious. Honestly, I haven't touched pizza since June. It was like I lost my taste for it after my parents told me about the move.

"I would eat pizza every day if my parents owned a pizza shop," Mikayla pipes up.

"I don't know, it's just not my favorite food," I say, and I'm relieved when the topic changes to the new Netflix show everyone is watching.

o ♥ o ♥ o

After school, the topic of pizza comes up again as Devin is walking with me to Soul Slice.

"So, if pizza isn't your favorite food, then what is?" she asks.

I give it some thought, watching the front wheel of my bike roll over the cracks in the sidewalk as I push it along. Since Devin lives past Soul Slice, we decided to walk together instead of me riding alone.

"I don't think I have one," I admit when nothing comes to mind.

"Oh, come on," Devin groans. "Everyone has a favorite food. Just think of something you really like and ask yourself if you've ever had anything as good as that."

My favorite food used to be the Corn Bread Crust pizza from Soul Slice. The crust was the perfect combination of spongy and fluffy. It was sweet with a little kick of cinnamon. To top it off, we'd make a whipped frosting flavored with canned yams in the mixer. If we were making it at home, Dad would always let me lick the spatula.

But that hasn't been my favorite for a while.

"It could be attached to a memory," Devin adds when I still don't come up with an answer.

I start mulling over good times that featured good foods, and one memory stands out from the rest.

"Family reunion when I was eight," I say.

"Tell me *everything*," Devin demands, holding out her fist like she's a reporter with a microphone.

"We were in Virginia. My family went down a few days early so we could stay at this water park before going to the reunion. Whenever we would stay in hotels, I'd collect brochures from the little kiosks by the elevators. So, one night, my parents had no idea where we should go to eat. I had this pamphlet for Captain George's Seafood Restaurant, and it was less than twenty minutes away. When I tell you it was bangin', I'm telling you it was *bangin'*."

Devin's eyes get wide, so I continue.

"The restaurant was nautical themed. There was a creek that flowed throughout that actually had little fish in it. And the buffet lines were boats! Even though it was a buffet, we still had a server, and since we weren't from the area, we didn't know what was good. She actually got the chef to come to our table, and he made recommendations, including"—I stop walking to drumroll on my bike's handlebars—"crayfish."

Devin's face falls, which I was expecting.

"No, though. Hear me out," I say, laughing a little. "They were so, so delicious. They were somehow salty but sweet, juicy but not overly so. And every morsel was different, but in a good way."

Every detail comes back to me. I remember sitting around the small table with my parents, surveying the piles of crab shells, shrimp tails, and my plate of picked-apart crayfish, feeling satisfied and happy. What made it a great memory was when Dad said this would be *our* spot, a place the three of us discovered together that we could always come back to. I felt close to them, way closer than I have in the past few weeks.

"So, if I *had* to pick, I'd say crayfish was my favorite food," I tell Devin.

Devin holds the "mic" up again, this time to herself. She nods silently for a moment, pretending to look out at a studio audience.

"Okay, we accept that answer. A lifetime supply of crayfish for you!"

"I'll smell like fish for the rest of my life."

We both burst out laughing.

"Your turn," I say once we've calmed down. "Favorite food."

"Okay, I know this makes it seem basic, but I liked this long before TikTok made it famous," she warns.

"By all means."

She takes a dramatic deep breath and says, "I *love* kimchi."

"Kimchi?"

"Kimchi."

I stare at her, though I know staring at her isn't going to suddenly help me figure out what kimchi is.

"You lost me," I have to admit.

"You don't know what kimchi is?" Devin asks, incredulous.

"Should I?"

"Well . . . yes! I mean, you used to live in *New York*."

"True," I relent. Given how diverse New York is, I should've at least *heard* about this food.

"It's a Korean dish," Devin explains. "It's basically cabbage fermented with an array of heavenly seasonings that transform it from a leaf into the greatest food ever."

"Cabbage?"

Seeing that I'm not catching on, Devin starts rubbing her temples in circles. "Hey, it's not like I picked a creepy-crawly thing."

"Might as well have," I kid.

"Promise me you'll try it."

"Promise," I say just as I roll my bike to a stop outside Soul Slice.

"So, this is the famous Soul Slice, come to town to take us by storm with soul food pizza," Devin says.

"I call it Soul Slice 2.0 because it's nothing like the original," I tell her. Devin gives me a half smile, and it helps to know someone empathizes with my frustration. "Do you want to come in and see?"

"Am I allowed, since it's not technically open?"

Even if she isn't, I'm sure I can swing the *I made a friend* angle and get my parents to let it go.

"Yeah, come on." I lean my bike against the front of the building and lead Devin inside. Watching her take it all in, I feel the need to explain. "The only reason that we are up and running for deliveries is because the kitchen is the first thing that was fully finished."

We make our way over to the cinder-block "counter," and Devin brushes her fingertips against the rough stone, still not giving away any thoughts she has about the space. She looks up at the wires dangling overhead. Her silence begins to make me uncomfortable.

"So, yeah, this is where my soul goes to die," I say, smiling sarcastically.

Devin brings her gaze down from the ceiling. "No way. Maya, this is so cool."

"Seriously?"

"There's so much you could do with this space. Do you guys have a color scheme?"

"Uh, I don't think so," I say, but then I remember what Mom said. "We do have an interior designer coming, though."

Suddenly, the front door opens, and when I look to see who's coming inside, my jaw drops.

No.

It's him again.

It's Justin.

chapter 5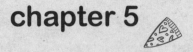

"What are *you* doing here?" I ask, incredulous. Did he *follow* me and Devin to Soul Slice? And how dare he just walk inside like *he* owns the place?

"Hello to you, too," Justin smirks, taking his backpack off and leaning it against the wall.

"No, no, no. Put that back on. You can't hang out here," I hiss.

"I'm not here to hang out, Maya. Would you just chill?"

I feel my eyebrows hit the roof as I stare at him in shock.

"Actually, *no*, I can't just 'chill,'" I mock him.

"Whatever. You're so uptight—"

"You wanna know what's 'uptight'?" I ask, feeling

all the confidence I lost when I tripped yesterday coming back to me.

I can hear Sasha's voice in the back of my head saying, *Tell him off, girl. This is your chance!*

"Uptight is someone who freaks out over the most honest mistake *anyone* could make and then blames *me* when I wasn't even the person who did it." Turning to Devin, I ask, "I mean, imagine listening to someone over a staticky phone. Doesn't pepperoncini sound like pepperoni?"

"Yes, it *does*," Devin says, having my back and turning to give Justin a much-deserved stank eye.

"*Okay*, I'm sorry," Justin says, holding up his hands.

"You've said that already," I remind him.

"Well, I am sorry! I was rude. I blamed you for a mistake that you didn't even make. And I didn't help you when you fell. There's no excuse."

"The fall wasn't your fault," I say, really not wanting his pity.

"It wasn't, but I still could've helped."

"And what would you have done, exactly?"

"Why can't you just accept the apology?" he asks, exasperated.

"Because *I'm sorry* doesn't fix it—"

"Incoming," Devin whispers, her eyes wide.

I turn around to see Mom approaching us from her office.

"Maya, you're not even clocked in. Where have you been?"

"I was talking to my friend Devin," I say, gesturing. "And trying to tell this young man that we aren't open yet and he can't stay here since the construction zone isn't safe." I turn around to give Justin a fake smile coupled with my death stare.

Mom grabs a hot bag and shuffles down to the convection ovens, where I can see more than three delivery orders waiting.

"I'm sorry, but construction aside, none of you can stay here. Maya has to work right now," Mom says, her tone apologetic even though I know she's not sorry— because if she was, *why would I be working!*

"Actually, I'm Justin Baker. Avery Baker's son," Justin says, stepping forward.

"Oh, my goodness," Mom says, suddenly flabbergasted. "Of course you can stay, Justin. Your dad should be here any minute."

Looking back and forth between them, I start to ask, "Why is his dad—"

But Mom cuts me off when she addresses Devin.

"Hello there. Can we help you?"

"Mom! That's my *friend* Devin, from school," I say, trying not to raise my voice to the impatiently "disrespectful" level.

"Oh my. I'm so embarrassed. My mind is all over the place right now." Mom wipes her hands on her jeans and then reaches out to shake Devin's hand. "I'm so glad Maya made a friend, and on her first day."

"Mom," I grumble, instantly regretting starting this interaction in the first place.

"Honey," she says, snapping from mom mode back into shop-owner mode. "These orders needed to be out of here ten minutes ago."

"What about Denise?" I ask, eyeing some of these addresses.

"Denise is out running deliveries. Maya, we need

you every day until the opening. I thought you under-stood that."

I understood that I was supposed to help out . . . I did *not*, as a matter of fact, understand that I was expected to work *every day*.

"Wait a second," I say, pausing. One new concern pokes through everything else going on. "Mom, I'm joining art club at school. It's on Wednesdays—"

"No," she says without blinking. "Maya, we need you *here*. End of discussion. Now, please, take these orders before we have to remake them." She gives me *the look*, and once she turns away, I am re-aware of the audience I have and feel self-conscious.

I avoid glancing at Justin, grab the orders, and head for the door with Devin at my side.

"Don't ride too fast, now," Justin teases before the door closes all the way.

Once Devin and I are on the street, words start vomiting out of my mouth.

"I mean, I know this restaurant opening is impor-tant for my parents, but it shouldn't mean I have to completely shut down my life. This isn't *my* business.

Moving here wasn't even my choice! Like, how can she expect me to make friends at a new school when I'm not allowed to hang out with anyone?"

My heart races, and I try to control my voice so that no one inside can hear me.

"Plus," I add, "you *see* what kind of luck I have? Like, what is *he* doing *here*?"

"That I'm not sure of. But in terms of shutting down your life, you might not have to," Devin says, her words slowing at the last part.

"What?"

"Come on, before your mom's eyes laser through the glass," Devin says, pointing to where Mom is standing behind the counter. When Mom catches my eye, she taps her watch.

I set the first address in my phone and start rolling my bike to the end of the street with Devin next to me. The thought that I might have to miss out on art club really sucks.

"What were you saying?" I ask Devin, holding on to my last bit of hope.

"I was saying there might still be a way for you to

do both, but I have to spend some time scheming."

It's not like I have any other options, so I say, "Whatever you come up with, I really hope it works."

"We shall see, we shall see," she says, bringing her fingertips together the way cartoon villains do when they're plotting. She breaks character to smile and adds, "It's not every day we get someone new, and I will not let that go to waste. Plus, you seem pretty cool and I *guess* we're friends now. I mean, your mom was so worried—"

"Shut. Up." We both break down laughing.

When we regain our composure, we say goodbye and split ways. I get on my bike and pick up momentum, thankful for the breeze and the temporary distraction. With one problem in Devin's hands, there's still another waiting for me back at Soul Slice—Justin.

○❤○❤○

When I get back from the deliveries, I find Mom checking the register.

"Good, you don't have anything up right now," she says, smiling at me. "We want you to meet the interior designer, Avery Baker. He's back in the office with his son and with Dad."

I set my hot bag on the counter, still a little out of breath from the hill I had to climb on my way back from the last delivery.

"Justin's dad, Avery, is the interior designer?" I ask, finally piecing it all together.

"Yup. And it sounds like you already met Justin at school."

"Is that what he told you?" I ask, a little sarcastic but hoping it comes off genuine enough that Mom won't detect it.

"Well, yes," she says. "He said you have English together."

Right. English, and the fact that he was rude to me and watched me face-plant into his front steps about twenty-four hours ago.

"We do," I say, ready to shift topics. "So, have you guys decided what you want the shop to look like?" I ask, pointing to the bare walls.

"We haven't decided anything, but we started brainstorming. Avery wants to hear some of your thoughts, too, so that he can put together some propositions."

"Really?" I ask. No one wanted my opinion on opening the store, but funny how they want my opinion on decorating . . .

"They're signing an official work agreement in the office. I told them I was going to check on you," Mom explains.

She pulls my cap off my head to inspect her handiwork with my hair. When she smiles, I can't help but smile a little.

"Good first day?" she asks, as if the tense conversation from earlier never happened.

"Yeah," I say, not wanting to bring the whole art club thing back up, at least not right now.

Suddenly, my dad, Justin, and a man about my dad's age who looks like a grown-up version of Justin emerge from the office. Mom introduces me to Mr. Avery, who at least seems friendlier than his son. Justin keeps glancing at me but not saying anything.

"I'm not sure how much weight my opinion carries, honestly," I admit when Mr. Avery asks me if I have any ideas.

"Maya, your ideas count. We want the store to reflect us as a family," Dad says.

"Right now, anything is fair game," Mr. Avery says, smiling.

Well, in that case . . .

"I think we should have soda machines on the far wall. Maybe include a few arcade games but not too many. That way we can get a lot of kids in the shop and not completely shut out adult customers. And I like the idea of a funky retro look. Like, work in a little bit of the *soul* that older customers might enjoy and younger customers will find trendy."

I watch, satisfied, as Dad picks his jaw up off the floor and Justin raises his eyebrows—surprised and probably impressed that, unlike him, I function off way more than two brain cells.

"Those are a lot of great points," Mr. Avery says, jotting down notes on his legal pad.

"I hadn't realized you'd given it this much thought," Mom admits.

Interior design has been a longtime love of mine. When I was little, I would take shoeboxes and pieces of cardboard and design "houses." Each box would be a room, and I would cut out squares and put in staircases, stacking the boxes to make apartments. Then I found my mom's ancient copy of the Sims game and went to town on our desktop. It wasn't until Dad walked by and saw that my Sim had a boy over—at her perfectly designed house, I must add—that he decided I was too young to play.

"Any more ideas?" Mr. Avery asks.

"None that I can think of," I tell him, catching Justin rolling his eyes. "But I'll be sure to let you know if anything comes up."

"Sounds like a plan," he says to me. Turning to my parents, Mr. Avery says, "Again, it was so nice to finally meet you guys. I can't wait to see Soul Slice come together."

After thanking him profusely, my parents walk him and Justin out.

Justin glances back at me, and I scowl at him. Just because my parents have to work with Mr. Avery doesn't mean I need to become friends with his son.

"Dear God, I know we haven't been to church in a minute, but you know I still gotchu," I say the next morning, kneeling down beside my bed, hands clasped in front of my heart the way MaMa taught me. "As you saw, the past few days have been . . . not good. Bad. *Terrible*. You get the picture."

I pause when I hear the floor creak outside my room. I crack open one eye and look over my shoulder, watching a shadow pass the opening at the bottom of my door. I wait until I hear the soft thud of footsteps on the stairs before I continue.

"So, yeah, I'm not a fan of the move. And I know MaMa says you don't give me stuff I can't handle, but this is pushing it. I mean, *child labor*?

"Like I said, I still think about you, and I have you in my heart. I don't swear, I try not to lie—most of the time—and I listen to my parents. So, please, please just lighten up. At least let today be better and let art club happen for me.

"Amen."

I take a deep breath and stand up. I haven't put a word in with the Big Guy since the end of last school year, when I was begging him to have mercy on my final exams. He came through, and since then, I've been so preoccupied with the mental gymnastics of convincing myself I wasn't going to end up in Hempstead that we've barely talked. My grandmother MaMa taught me that when you have a load, God can take it off your hands. So, here's hoping.

I grab my backpack and my math homework off my desk. With my hand on the doorknob, the rest of day number two waiting on the other side, I realize I forgot something.

"Oh, and let Sasha be okay, too. Thanks."

At the bottom of the stairs, I stop to check myself in the full-length mirror. I have on another pair of jean shorts, this time with my brown leather belt. Today, my batik shirt is sleeveless, with hot-pink leaf outlines dyed into navy-blue fabric. It's one of my favorites, and it's been washed so many times that it's starting to fade.

While I use a hair tie to put the top half of my braids up in a bun, the memory of Waverly crossing the cafeteria with Justin flashes through my mind. Evil twin or not, she's undeniably beautiful. Like, really pretty. *Maybe Justin would be nicer to me if I looked like that.*

I shake my head, pushing that stupidly insecure thought away. MaMa would say something generic and cheesy but perfectly applicable—like *Everyone is beautiful in their own way* or *Your beauty is unique to you.* I can even picture her stitching this onto a pillow.

Plus, what Justin thinks about me is the *last* thing I care about.

Following the scent of butter and waffles, I wander into the kitchen. I hang my backpack over my chair and sit down to a fixed plate, completely unnoticed.

"Maybe we can try a dark green paired with a light blue," Mom proposes before taking a swig of her coffee. She absentmindedly hands the mug to me, letting me take a sip.

"I don't know. We'd be repeating green from the previous shop, and I want to go for something new," Dad says through a mouthful of doughy waffle.

While listening, I reach for the syrup and pour diligently into the little squares of my waffle. Then I grab my fork and knife and start cutting out each little syrup-filled pocket, perfectly bite-size with the perfect amount of sweetness.

"Maybe we could try bright colors? Kids are into pink," Mom says. She snatches the coffee away when I try to sneak another sip.

"Why are you trying and failing at pairing colors together?" I ask, figuring I might as well be included if I can't be ignored enough to have coffee.

Dad opens his mouth, but when he takes a breath, he immediately starts choking.

"This is why you shouldn't talk with your mouth full," Mom says, rolling her eyes.

Dad reaches for her cup of coffee and takes a few gulps. When he sets the mug down on the table, the sign that he's officially okay, Mom takes it over to the counter, where there's still half a pot of coffee waiting to be had.

"We're trying to pick a color scheme for the shop," Dad says, wiping his mouth with a napkin.

"Oh."

"Yup, we have to figure that out so that we can buy paint and start picking out furniture," Mom explains, coming back to the table.

"And you were thinking blue and green?" I ask, laughing a little.

"Not all of us are aspiring artists," Dad teases, spearing some of his waffle and swirling it in a pool of syrup and crumbs.

"Yeah, we had no idea you had so much insight for this kind of stuff," Mom adds, spooning some sugar into her mug.

"Really?" I'm surprised that between all the interior design YouTube videos I watched and the homemade dollhouses that it flew over their heads.

"We knew that you liked making things, but hearing you bring it home yesterday in our actual shop—"

"Yeah, and not in a shoebox," Dad adds, chuckling.

"That just surprised us," Mom finishes.

I stand up, knowing I won't get any more coffee and needing something to wash down breakfast. Reflexively, I reach for the cabinet above the sink. But with my hand on the knob, I remember the new spot for cups.

"Well," I say, thinking as I fill my cup with water from our new filtered sink. I look at the faded, chipped confetti pattern on the side of the cup, feeling like I'm holding every single time I've used this cup since I was five or six in this moment now. With so much change, I'm still somewhat amazed at how our old stuff fits so perfectly in the new kitchen—in this new life.

"Well what, Maya?" Mom prompts.

I go back to my seat, the same place I always sit, with Dad at the head of the table and Mom across from me. In our old kitchen, we had a cabinet behind Dad's seat where my parents kept the fancy holiday dishes. Among the finer dinnerware was a teapot, gifted to us from Mom's mom in Italy. It was the ugliest teapot I've ever seen, purple with orange flowers—like something out of the seventies. But Nonna thought it was a treasure and gifted it to my parents.

One summer, my parents elected to host Dad's side of the family in New York for their reunion. My baby cousin, Chanel, thought it would be fun to have a tea party with some of the dolls she stole from my room, and . . . well, anyone can guess what happened from there.

Now that I'm thinking about it, as ugly as it was, the teapot was weirdly pretty, too. It was funky. It was bold and commanded your attention. Like, you couldn't walk through the dining room without noticing the purple or pop of orange out of the corner of your eye. And maybe that's just what Soul Slice 2.0 needs. A soulful purple, a funky bright orange, and a piece of our Italian heritage woven in.

"What about orange and purple?" I ask. "Like a deep purple complemented with a bright—but not, like, highlighter-bright—orange."

Mom and Dad look at each other, Mom's index finger circling the mouth of her mug and Dad's chin resting in his hand.

"I like it," Dad says after a moment, nodding.

"We can run it by Avery this afternoon," Mom says, adding, "so, please don't be late today. We don't want to have to worry about you while we're in these meetings."

Right. Of course . . .

"Don't worry, Mom. I'll be there," I say before spearing four squares of waffle and shoving them into my mouth, suddenly ready for breakfast to be over.

When I wheel my bike through our gate, an idea hits me. The festival, all the new art supplies at school, the blank canvas of the shop, and my love of interior design; I know what my project for the art festival can be! Excitement zips through me as designs for a mini version of Soul Slice 2.0 start materializing in my mind. I whip out my phone and jot down a few ideas before I forget them. Then I shove my phone back into my pocket and get on my way to school.

chapter 6

When I find Justin hovering outside our English class-room, I nearly stop short and duck into the girls' room. But he sees me.

"Hey, Maya," he says, reaching out and touching my arm to stop me from going inside.

"What?" I ask, shifting away from his hand.

"We should meet up after school and walk to Soul Slice together."

"I already walk with Devin," I say, stiffening.

"Well, I can walk with you guys."

"Why?"

Justin scrunches up his brows, probably confused as to why I'm not dying to have the chance to walk with him and his uppity khakis.

"My dad wants me to start walking you to the shop."

Okay, not what I was expecting.

"*Why?*" I repeat, squinting with suspicion. "Does he think I can't get there on my own or something?"

"I honestly don't know, he just told me to start walking with you. So, after school we should meet—"

The bell rings, and I head straight for my desk. Of course, Justin sits right across from me so I don't exactly escape him.

"Look, I'm sorry—" he starts to say.

"I don't need your pity, okay? It was an accident. I'm sorry for being rude. You're sorry for being rude. I got my karma. You don't have to walk me to work. You don't have to pretend you like me. I just want to pretend nothing ever happened. It's already hard enough being the new kid."

My last sentence kind of just slips out, but nevertheless it's true. I just wasn't planning on sharing anything sincere with Justin.

Thankfully, Mrs. Moore likes to get into her lessons immediately and leaves no room for Justin to try and keep talking. Unfortunately, Justin finds his way around that and slides his notebook halfway across the table, far enough that it's not obvious what he's doing but close enough that I can read his scribbled handwriting on the top corner of his page.

Can we start over?

Honestly, starting over is the last thing I want to do. I started over a few days ago when I got here, and Justin ruined that. But I know that if I don't give him a second chance, then I'll be holding a grudge for at least a year, maybe more if we end up with another class together next year . . .

I shrug, hoping to convey *maybe*, and motion for Justin to pay attention to Mrs. Moore before we get caught.

o ♥ o ♭ o

"Do you have any ideas for how to get me into art club?" I ask Devin on our way to the art room for lunch.

"Not yet, but I'm still scheming," she says, pulling her bag of BBQ Fritos out of her backpack.

"It's okay if you don't think of anything," I say, just to make sure she knows. "I'd understand, especially given the short notice."

We shoulder our way against the current of students, heading away from the cafeteria to the stairwell that'll take us down to the art wing.

"Don't be so quick to give up!" Devin calls to me when a few people get between us.

I instantly feel ten times better when Devin and I duck inside Mr. Chris's room. Mr. Chris seems pretty laid-back. He wears a flannel shirt and jeans and has a pair of glasses that primarily live on his forehead instead of in front of his eyes. His art room is a vibe, and it's not uncommon for students to hang out there during lunch or after school on non-club days.

Devin introduces me to Mr. Chris. I quickly explain about being new to the school and wanting to join art club and enter a project in the festival, to which he says, "Great, help yourself." That's it. He gives me a polite smile before leaning back in his chair and plopping a huge pair of headphones over his ears. He starts bobbing his head to whatever he's listening to.

"He usually reads the school newspaper, but nothing has been released yet," Devin tells me as we set our lunch bags down on a table.

I pull my sketchbook out of my binder and slip my graphite pencil out of my pen case. Devin reaches into one of the cubbies behind us and pulls out a gallon-size Ziploc bag more than half full and fat with . . . paper clippings.

"Is this for your project?" I ask when she starts pulling out magazine cutouts from the bag and spreading them across the table.

"Yeah," she says, smiling to herself. With her head tilted down, her pink cupcake earrings—meant to match her bright pink-and-white zebra-print jumpsuit— dangle against her cheeks.

"May I ask what you're working on, or are you more secretive about your work?" I ask, wanting to respect her process. At my old school, some of the other kids were pretty weird about sharing their ideas before they had a final product.

"Oh, no. I'm happy to share. It's a collage of me."

"A collage of you?" I ask, peering over at the halo of yellow-and-brown intricacies surrounding her container of macaroni salad.

"Well, it's going to be. I've been collecting cutouts all summer. I'm nervous I won't have enough."

"It looks like you might have plenty," I tell her, genuinely impressed with the amount she's collected. I mean, I've collaged before, but I don't think I've even looked at enough magazines to see the number of pictures she's cut out.

"It's, like, a *big* collage," she warns, something frantic coming into her eyes.

"Well, do you need more magazines? We get some mailed to the shop—my parents don't care about them."

Devin pauses, reaching out and grabbing my right shoulder. "This is destiny, you and me. We were meant to be friends," she says, the huge smile on her face contagious.

We set to work. I sketch between bites of my turkey sandwich, and Devin sorts between forkfuls of macaroni salad, the quiet chewing a perfect white noise for concentration. Halfway through lunch, I have a few solid rough sketches of what I envision the front of Soul Slice 2.0 to look like.

"I guess the next step is figuring out what to use to actually build it," I say, thinking out loud.

Devin breaks her concentration and leans over to look at my sketches.

Before she can say what she thinks, someone says, "Why can't you eat lunch in the cafeteria like a normal person?"

We both look up and find Waverly floating into the room, Justin in tow. *Ugh.* Is there no escaping him?

"What do you want?" Devin asks her sister.

"Mom told me to have you text her on my phone since yours isn't working," Waverly says, her voice an annoyed hiss. She hands Devin her phone, holding on to it for a moment and adding, "Be quick."

Looking at them together is a little trippy. They look exactly alike—which makes sense, since they're identical twins. Still, they're so different that it almost feels wrong that they look the same.

"Hey," Justin says, his voice quiet.

"Hey," I say, trying to shrug off the awkward feeling coming over me.

"Nice drawings," he says, pointing at my sketches. I know he's saying it to be polite, but after *actually* glancing at the paper, Justin does a double take and comes closer, leaning over my shoulder. "Are these of Soul Slice?"

Even though Devin was looking at them not even five minutes ago, suddenly I feel self-conscious. I wonder if he thinks I'm a good artist from these sketches alone; then I wonder if *I'm* a good artist from these sketches alone. Then I notice a few places where my lines could be cleaner and resist the urge to go over them with my eraser.

When Justin doesn't say anything, I look up. His honey-brown eyes are darting back and forth, taking their time.

Waverly comes around Devin on my other side, and without asking, she picks up my sketchbook to look closer at the drawing.

"Can I have that back, please?" I mumble, pulling the book out of her hands.

"Your ideas were really good yesterday," Justin finally says, which—for whatever reason—makes me feel relieved.

"Thanks."

"So, are you—like—helping your parents design the shop? Or . . . ?"

"This is just my project for the art festival—"

"Ugh, your shirt is giving me a headache," Waverly interrupts.

I whip around, shocked. She's standing maybe a step behind me, leaning back and rubbing her temples.

"Excuse me?" I ask her.

"What's *wrong* with you?" Devin asks, making a face that Waverly then mimics to her.

"Just take an aspirin." Justin says it like it's nothing, like that's the natural flow of conversation. He leans back down to look at my sketches, like Waverly's jab was a minor annoyance and not, in fact, an insult.

Waverly just rolls her eyes and picks at a clump of mascara in her lashes.

"You should show these to your parents, or at least to my dad," Justin tells me.

Still confused, surprised, and stuck in the previous moment, my brain takes a second to catch up. Share my art with my parents? Share my doodle ideas for the shop with an actual interior designer? No thank you!

"It's just a project for the festival," I say, closing my book. "I'm sure your dad's ideas are way better than this."

When I look up, Justin is looking right at me. For a second, I can't look away from his eyes even though I want to.

"Here. Leave *now*. Please!" Devin shoves Waverly's phone back into her hands. "You're disrupting the creative process."

"Come on," Waverly demands, tugging Justin's arm and leading him back out of the art room.

"See you, Maya," he calls before they disappear through the door frame.

"So, he works at Soul Slice, too, now?" Devin asks, bobbing her eyebrows suggestively.

"He does *not*," I assure her. "My mom said his dad is teaching him stuff."

Devin scrunches up her face, confused. "Teaching him *what* stuff?"

"Interior design. Like, he's teaching him how to do what he does."

Devin squints, looking away from her project and up at the ceiling in thought. "Why?"

"Do I look like I know why Avery does what he does?" I ask, feeling a little incredulous.

"Oh, *Avery*," Devin says, dragging out his name. "You're on a first-name basis."

"Gross," I say, picking up one of her cutouts and throwing it at her.

"Not as gross as Waverly trying to insult a fire tee," Devin says as-a-matter-of-fact-ly, gesturing to my batik tee.

"It was a weak attempt," I say, glad to have Devin.

"Justin's comeback, though . . ." she says. "I'd call *that* redeemable."

Me too, I think to myself, not sure if I'm willing to admit it out loud just yet.

"Okay, so even though you're all pizza-ed out, I want your honest opinion," Devin says that afternoon as we leave school together.

"Opinion on what?" I ask. I free my bike from the rack and start wheeling it alongside Devin.

"What are the top Soul Slice specialty pizzas? Like, if I was going to order something, what would you recommend?"

A perfectly valid question that I honestly haven't considered in a while.

"Uh," I say, running down the menu in my brain. As the daughter of Soul and Slice, I know it by heart. But deciding on the *best* items takes something deeper than a photographic memory.

"And I'm talking about your soul food pizzas," Devin adds. "I know you guys make regular pizzas, but I want to know about the ones that gave the shop its name."

"Right . . ." I say. "Okay. There's the Fried Chicken and Waffle pizza—the perfect combination of sweet and savory with a light drizzle of maple syrup on top for added originality. There's our Corn Bread Crust pizza, the Mom's Mac 'n' Cheese—which is basically pizza with all the cheeses you use in mac 'n' cheese sprinkled with breadcrumbs. The Southern BBQ pizza with a home-made sauce . . . oh! And the Biscuits and Gravy pizza. That one has a biscuit-like crust that crumbles, a thin layer of cheese and no red sauce, and is topped with smoky collard greens and turkey drizzled in gravy."

Devin stops walking and stares at me with her mouth hanging open.

"You've been sitting on *that* gold mine the *whole* time we've known each other and didn't say a word?" She shriek-screams the whole sentence.

I laugh, realizing that her "gold mine" is just the pizza my parents make. It's unique, don't get me wrong, but it's the pizza I've grown up eating. Though I guess our soul food pizzas are new to Devin, and to Hempstead.

"I'm sorry, Dee. I've just been all over the place; it didn't cross my mind," I tell her.

"'Dee,'" she repeats, pensively tucking a green strand of hair behind her ear. "I like that. It's cool, clipped, and mysterious."

Mysterious? I decide to let her have that.

"Guys!" someone shouts from behind us.

We both turn around, having nearly made it off school grounds, and find Justin running and waving us down.

"Come on, where were we?" I say, continuing to push my bike.

"Wait!" Justin shouts.

"Maya, I think he's talking to us."

"He is," I say. "So, how big is your collage—"

"Hold on," Devin says, now a few steps behind me since she hasn't moved.

Unfortunately, Justin catches up to us and immediately doubles over with his hands on his knees, trying to catch his breath.

"Look what you did," I hiss to Devin.

She gives me a confused look before asking, "Where's the fire?"

Justin shakes his head and stands up straight, still breathing heavy. "I told you we have to walk together."

"*We* don't have to do anything," I correct him, all three of us finally falling back in step. "If your dad tells you to do something, that has nothing to do with me."

"What did your dad tell you to do?" Devin asks.

"He wants me to walk with Maya to Soul Slice after school."

"Oh, well, that makes sense," Devin says.

"It does?" we both ask, accidentally at the same time.

I glare at Justin before focusing back on Devin and her crazy logic.

"Well, instead of your dad coming to pick you up," she says to Justin, "you'll all just meet at the shop."

Justin shrugs. With Devin here, I don't want to act rude or get in my feelings and do something embarrassing, so I drop it.

When we reach the shop, Devin breaks the silence to say, "That was the most awkward walk *ever*. Can't wait to do it again tomorrow."

"See you," Justin says.

"See ya!" Devin says to him, and then to me she quirks her eyebrow and says, "I'll pray you don't kill anyone before the day is over."

"Funny," I say, monotone.

Inside, I go behind the counter, clock in, and open

the cabinet under the delivery station to shove my backpack inside.

"Hold up," Justin says before I close the cabinet door all the way.

"What are you doing back here?"

"I was going to put my stuff away, too," he says, all innocent.

"You're not an employee. You're not supposed to be back here."

"Oh." His shoulders sag and his face falls, and for a second, he turns from a rude wannabe G to a, like, puppy. UGH!

I snatch his bag, which is light—figures, since he acts like he's never learned anything—and shove it into the cabinet with mine.

With our stuff secure, I click onto the delivery screen to see the upcoming orders. Denise is out running one right now, and a few are coming up due for me.

"So, how do you, like, make the pizzas?"

I jump, startled.

"You're still here?"

"Why are you so rude?" Justin asks, leaning all his weight against the counter and crossing his arms. *Oh no, so much sass. What ever shall I do?*

"Maybe because you were rude first."

He scoffs.

"Maya, why can't you just accept my apology and get over it? I said I'm sorry!"

"Because *I'm sorry* doesn't fix it. *Sorry* is all I've been hearing for weeks, and it hasn't done *anything*," I say, my voice beginning to rise.

I catch myself, not wanting to drop any more of my baggage onto him. I take a deep breath and press my face into my hands.

"Look, I accept your apology. I'm sorry if I was rude to you, too. So, let's just move on." I keep my hands over my face because this little bit of peace I've found is really refreshing and I also don't want to see the expression on Justin's face after I admit that I possibly, maybe, hypothetically could share some blame.

"Good, you're here!"

I look up and see Justin's dad standing in the doorway of the shop. He's wearing a suit and tie but also has on a hard hat. Two more hard hats are awkwardly under his arms and the other one is dangling from his index finger. Justin goes to him and I watch as he pulls the hat on, probably dreading what it's going to do to his waves.

My parents come out of the office to greet Justin's dad. Meanwhile, I watch the delivery monitor like a hawk, ready to get out of here.

Of course, when I hear my name getting tossed around, I emerge from behind the counter to see what's going on.

"Maya actually recommended those colors," Mom is saying when I come up behind my parents.

"They're unconventional, but I think they'll really pop," Mr. Avery says.

"Here's our little in-house designer herself," Dad says, resting his arm over my shoulders. "Do you have any more ideas that you want to run by us?"

"Nope," I say, smiling politely.

"That's not true," Justin says, looking genuinely confused.

All eyes shift to him, and with the attention off me,

I give him my best *You better not* glare, hoping he can read my mind.

"I mean, I hope it's not," he corrects himself, looking away from me. "I'm sure you'll have more good ideas."

"Thanks," I say, regretting coming over here in the first place only to make things awkward. "I'm going to go check on the orders," I tell my parents, excusing myself.

I catch Denise at the delivery station, bagging her next orders.

"Please let me take one of these," I whisper, grabbing the bag before she can lift it off the counter.

Startled, Denise jerks back. "These are too far. Your mom won't want you riding your bike that much," Denise tells me.

"Please," I beg. "I *have* to get out of here."

Her face softens, shifting from confused to amused. She peers around the corner of the delivery station, at where my parents and the Bakers are still deep in their meeting.

"Trouble in paradise?" she asks, returning her focus to me.

"If by *paradise* you mean everything that's going wrong in my life right now, then yes." When she doesn't seem to budge, I add, "And you can still keep the tip. I don't care."

This makes her laugh. "Girl, there is no way your life is *that* bad."

Try me.

She sighs, checking her receipts and handing one to me. She unzips her delivery bag and pulls out one of the boxes. I reach for it, but she doesn't let go, forcing me to look up at her.

"Keep the tip. Take the order because I have your back, *not* because life sucks. And ride fast. Don't get me in trouble."

"Deal," I say, never happier to have my job.

chapter 7

That night, after I shower, eat dinner, and do my homework, I finally can call Sasha and catch her up on everything that's been going on. I've texted her about how I met Justin (and fell into his pizza) and how he's always at Soul Slice now, but it feels good to really *talk* about it. I also tell her about art club, and Sasha says she's rooting for me to find a way to go.

By the end of the school day on Wednesday, all I can think about is how I'm going to get to art club. I really don't want to miss it and lose my spot in the festival, especially now that I've developed my idea. But Devin still hasn't come up with a workable scheme.

I'm distracted as I walk to Soul Slice that afternoon, Justin a few paces behind me. Thinking as fast as

I can, I figure my best bet might be convincing Denise to let me take one of her orders again. I can try to catch one that goes past the school, ride my bike really fast, and then use the extra time to stop into art club—at least to sign my name on the attendance sheet.

When we arrive at the shop, I pull the door open and step back, gesturing for Justin to go through.

"No, you go," he says, reaching over my head to hold the door for me.

"No, it's cool. Go on," I say, not moving.

"I got it. Go inside," he insists, smiling at me and shaking his head.

I relent, mumbling, "Thank you" under my breath as I duck inside.

Since Mr. Avery is already here, I hold out my hand and take Justin's backpack with me behind the counter. I'm relieved that Denise isn't here because it gives me free rein over the orders. I clock in, checking my phone to see that art club officially starts in fifteen minutes. I sneak around the corner from the delivery station to the oven and look inside.

"How many orders is this?" I ask Jean.

"Just the one right now," he says, back turned to me as he stays focused on the pizza in front of him.

"That's five pizzas," I say, feeling a pit begin to form in my stomach.

"Yeah?"

"Cool," I say, though it comes sailing out on a long sigh.

I'm not supposed to carry more than two pizzas— three or four if they're all smalls—at a time. Five medium pizzas! I'll look like an incompetent dork if I have to make multiple trips for one order, and it would undoubtedly put me behind.

I decide not to let this break me. I think I can make the huge delivery in one long trip if I'm being super careful while balancing a stack on my bike. And that would mean I could swing by the school and be back by a reasonable enough time that my parents wouldn't be suspicious.

Once the first three pizzas are boxed, I slip them into a delivery bag. I head outside with the first bag and secure it to my bike carrier. I barely catch what Justin's dad is talking about with my parents when I pass through the front of the store. They're standing on the far side under an unfinished part of the ceiling. Hopefully they're talking about finishing it because that's one of the biggest eyesores in this place.

With them occupied, no one notices me come back in and get the rest of the order.

Outside, the sun still beating down, I set the bag on top of the other and start figuring out how to tie the straps so that it's secured enough that the order won't fall off if I make a sharp turn or hit a bump. Once I know they're as good as they're going to get, I program the address into my phone, thankful that it's not too far. I'm gonna have to ignore my intuition telling me this is a horrible idea or else I'll be sick.

"Maya."

Sitting on my bike, heel poised to kick the stand, I whip around and see Dad and Mom filing out the door with Justin and his dad in tow.

"Hey," I say, because there's no hiding the fact that I'm doing something wrong.

"What are you doing?" Dad asks.

"Making deliveries?"

"You have too many. You have to make multiple trips," Dad says. "You know this."

The way he's looking at me, you'd think I have a horn sticking out of my forehead.

"This is all one order," I say. "I'm trying to be efficient."

"Maya, that's not safe," Mom chimes in.

I mean, she's not *wrong*.

"How close is the delivery address?" Justin's dad asks, making my parents turn their heads around like owls.

"Um, just a couple blocks away . . ." I say slowly, not sure if he's helping or hurting my situation.

"Why doesn't Justin help? If it's close, you guys could walk the order together?"

Definitely hurting the situation, DEFINITELY HURTING!

"Yeah, I don't mind," Justin adds, looking at my parents and not me, probably because he can guess that I'd try to melt his brain with my eyes.

Dad scratches his head, and Mom looks at him, then at me, and back to him.

Please say no. Please say no.

"Okay, maybe just this once," Dad relents.

I silently wonder why God has forsaken me, but I don't have much time to dwell on the question. I untie my almost disaster and hand one of the delivery bags off to Justin, hoping that this doesn't end with me diving face-first into another mess.

"This would be way faster if we had a car," Justin says behind me.

"No duh." I'm beginning to wonder if the light weight of his backpack is a testament to the light weight of his brain.

"At least we get to be outside, though. I mean, it's a beautiful day."

Instead of asking if we're really going to make small talk the whole way, I say, "I personally would rather not have to do this at all."

"Yeah, it must be a lot. Moving, working, and starting at a new school."

I slow down, just a tiny unnoticeable bit, and let Justin catch up with me.

"It's been a change," I say slowly.

"All for a good cause," Justin adds, lightly drumming on top of his bag. He has his strap lengthened all the way so that it loops around his back and he can wear the delivery bag like a boxy fanny pack.

"I just hope that after the grand opening everything goes back to some version of normal," I admit, checking my phone to see how we're doing on time.

"It will," he says confidently.

I laugh a little. "How do you know?"

"It's like metaphoric homeostasis," he explains. "Right now, things are so out of whack that it's hard for you to function. Your system—which in this case is your life and how you move through it—is itching to get back to a state of equilibrium—your version of normal. All these elements making things hard aren't part of everyday life; they are like a virus that entered your body and now your body is trying to get back to a state of health. Does that make sense?"

"Yes," I say, trying not to sound too surprised. So, maybe stuff is happening up in his brain after all. "Thanks for, like, validating me or whatever."

"Of course."

I relent that there's more to Justin than I was initially led—by him—to believe.

"Why do you dress like that?" I ask, adjusting the strap on my bag so it's not digging a groove into my shoulder.

"Like what?"

"The way you do, like you're trying so hard to be . . ." I trail off, not wanting to say it.

"Well, why do you dress the way you do?" he asks.

"It expresses my personality," I explain.

"I was going to ask you where you got your shirts from," Justin admits. "And if they make any for guys. The prints are cool."

"My mom makes them," I tell him.

"Really?"

I look over and see his face lit up.

"Yeah?"

"That's awesome. I don't think my mom could do that."

"Well, if you don't know how to sew, then you don't know how to sew."

"They're really cool," Justin says.

The compliment washes over my skin, making me feel warm—or warmer than I already am. "Thanks," I say. "I like these shirts because they're colorful, cultured, and artistic. The fabric has a story, and the fact that my mom makes them for me—to fit me specifically—makes them unique. So, what about you? A white T-shirt and khakis don't give away much about your personality."

"Says who?" Justin challenges, quirking his brow. Looking at his smile from the left side, I notice that one of his teeth is just a tiny bit crooked—also unique.

"So, your personality is plain?" I say, mocking his tone.

"Maybe my personality is *personal*, and instead of giving it away with clothes, I keep it hidden until people get to know me."

I shake my head, laughing a little again. "You are *not* that deep."

"You are not *that* mean," Justin says, which makes us both laugh. "Speaking of you being *nice*," he adds, not missing a beat, "I was hoping you could tell me how you guys make your pizzas."

"Why?"

"I've never made pizza before, and I actually love cooking."

"Really?" I ask, this time not hiding my surprise. Then again, he does have the last name *Baker*.

"Yeah, it's, like, my secret passion," he admits, following my lead as I jump over a now-familiar hole in the sidewalk.

"Why is it a secret?" I ask.

Before he can answer, I notice the GPS on my phone has indicated we've arrived at the delivery spot. I look up, and we're in front of our *school*. I stop abruptly, Justin bumping into me.

"What is it?" he asks, looking at my GPS over my shoulder.

"Are we delivering these pizzas to school?" I ask. I squint at the faded type on the receipt, searching for the address.

"Looks like it," he says, pointing at the tiny type and then shifting his finger over to the identical address on the screen, which is flagged by a red dot over our middle school.

We start up the driveway, the same way I come and go every day.

"This doesn't make sense," I say. "How are we supposed to know where these are going? There isn't a room number or anything."

We'll be so wrapped up knocking on every classroom door to search for the customer that I'll miss art club altogether.

"Over here!" a familiar voice shouts.

We scan the schoolyard until we see someone waving us down from a side entrance, holding the door open with their foot.

"Is that Waverly's sister?" Justin asks.

"No way!"

I feel weightless, running as fast as I can while keeping the pizza boxes level in my arms. Devin gives me a knowing nod and steps to the side, holding the door open wide enough for Justin and me to fit through with our bags.

"This was your plan?" I ask as Devin takes my bag from me.

She nods, beaming. "I wasn't sure if the school was

technically close enough for you to be assigned the order, so I didn't want to get your hopes up. But I'm so glad it worked!" she gushes.

"Me too! You should've warned me that you're a genius."

We follow Devin as she leads us down the hall. Never having used that entrance before, I realize it's dropped us right in the art wing.

Just as we're about to head into Mr. Chris's room, Justin stops me.

"Don't we have to get back to Soul Slice?"

I pretend to check my watch before saying, "Well, we made good enough time. We might as well have a slice."

Justin nods, not in agreement but like he's seeing through everything I just said.

I add, "Look, this is the first art club meeting and this is the only way that I'll be able to attend. Do you really *want* to go back to the shop now?" I remember him looking bored while listening to his dad talk about interior design and decide to bank on it.

"Art club it is," he says, moving past me to follow Devin.

This is the first time I've seen Mr. Chris's room filled with students. Mikayla and Sophie come to the front of the room to help us set up the pizza boxes. There are already bottles of soda on a table along with Solo cups and paper plates.

"Everyone!" Devin announces, capturing the attention of the room. "This is Maya. Her family owns the new pizza shop." I wave to the room, feeling a little shy.

When Devin opens the first box of pizza, she loses her concentration and so does everyone else. It's a Fried Chicken and Waffle pizza, and the unleashed aromas pull everyone to the front table. All the boxes fly open to reveal the rest of our signature pizzas. Soon, everyone is seated again with one or two slices.

"I don't know which one to try," Justin admits when Devin turns to us, offering paper plates. He looks to me for guidance.

"Either the Biscuits and Gravy or the Fried Chicken and Waffle," I say.

Devin gives him one of each, and I make a plate with a slice of BBQ chicken. Even though BBQ is my personal favorite, it's not always my first recommendation for someone looking to really experience a Soul Slice slice.

"Do you want a napkin?" Justin asks, though he's already reaching for one.

I say, "Thanks," feeling grateful and a little impressed.

"Oh, my goodness," Sophie says through a mouthful of Mom's Mac 'n' Cheese.

"I know, right?" Mikayla adds before taking a sip of her soda to wash down her Corn Bread Crust.

"Maya, this is, like, amazing," Devin swoons, savoring her Fried Chicken and Waffle slice.

"For real," Justin chimes in. "You *have* to teach me how to make this."

I look over at him, chewing his slice of Biscuits and Gravy with his eyes closed, vibing with the flavors. I take my first bite, and somehow, even though I've had this pizza a million times—on its best and worst days—it tastes perfect and new.

After enjoying a slice of Mom's Mac 'n' Cheese, Mr. Chris begins the lesson. The first half of club meetings are a short lecture, and the second half is when students have a chance to practice what they learn. Keeping it simple for the first meeting, Mr. Chris talks about sketching.

"It's important to keep your wrist loose and let the lines take their own shape. Sketching isn't the same as drawing. Your sketch is like a rough draft, and drafts aren't meant to be perfect. The lines should be light, not definitive."

As he gives an example on the huge sketch pad he has propped up on an easel, Mikayla passes me the attendance sheet and a pen.

I mouth, *Thank you*, before signing my name.

When Mr. Chris says everyone can get to work on their own sketches, I nudge Justin, and we seize the opportunity to slip out in the momentary chaos. I'm glad I was at least able to catch the first part of the meeting.

Exiting the building back out into the heat, my skin buzzes from the sunshine and from the surprise of showing up, thinking all was lost, only to see that Devin had my back in the best, most unimaginable way.

"Maybe art club can order pizzas again next

Wednesday," I say, more to myself than to Justin. "And maybe I can stay at the meeting even longer . . ." The plan is so simple, and feeding a whole club is good business for Soul Slice, anyway.

"So, I was thinking," Justin says as we speed-walk back to Soul Slice.

"Were you, now?"

"Do your parents know you're going to go to art club?"

I feel like this is heading in a direction that I'm not entirely sure of yet.

"No," I say, keeping my tone even.

"So, it's a secret?"

Gosh, he's making this hard.

"Yes," I say.

"How much is it worth to you?"

"*That* sounds like a threat," I say, using the back of my hand to wipe a single bead of sweat trickling down from my hairline.

"No, no. Not a threat . . . more like brokering a deal," he says, trying and failing to sound innocent.

I slow down so that he can catch up. When

he does, I see his forehead glistening with sweat.

"And here I was, beginning to think you're a decent human being," I hiss, trying to ignore the nerves ricocheting around my stomach like it's a racquetball court.

I should've kept my guard up. Justin isn't trustworthy, and now he has a new thing to snitch on me for. Why didn't I think *that* through?

"Hey, I'm just trying to come up with a way for both of us to be winners."

"By *threatening* me?" I speed up again, not wanting to even see his dishonest ulterior-ly motivated face out of the corner of my eye. "We both *win* by me going to art club and staying happy enough not to snap at you."

"That's not really a win for me."

"Where did this idea of *winning* even come from? Why do you have to win?" I demand, exasperated.

Soul Slice comes into view up ahead. I sigh. Art club was great, and seeing everything come together so cleanly—in a way that'll be easy to do over next week and hopefully every week until the grand opening— would make missing it now not only the worst thing *ever*, but it would also make me feel like a failure.

But with Justin dangling my own fate over my head and only one block left before said fate is sealed, I realize there might not be a *next week's meeting*. We have to hash this conversation out all the way, right here. Right now.

I grab Justin by the wrist—because, *ew*, not going to hold hands with a grimy scheming backstabber—and drag him over to the wall of the hardware store. This way, no one inside Soul Slice can see us.

"You could've just said *Come here*," Justin says, amused.

"What do you want?" I cross my arms. We're already late getting back, and putting art club in jeopardy isn't my idea of funny.

"I propose that I'll keep your art club secret if you teach me how to make pizza."

"What is it with you and learning how to make pizza?" I ask, incredulous.

"I like cooking," Justin says. "And I love pizza."

I shrug. "When would I even teach you? I work here after school, and after work I have homework, and after homework I need to work on my art project—"

"But you do have *some* time," he interrupts, quirking a brow. "How about Saturday?"

He's got me there. I don't really have any big plans on Saturday other than my evening shift at Soul Slice.

"Come on, Maya," he adds. "Teach me how to make pizza, and your secret is safe with me. And I'm not asking you to spend the whole day with me, or even a whole hour. You can teach me bits and pieces when you have time."

"You really want to make pizza *that* bad?" I ask, taking my turn to be amused.

Justin looks me in the eye for a moment and then presses his hands against his face. I can't tell if he's frustrated or finding this funny.

"You have your art, and there's a club that you can go to, to do it with other people and learn how to get better. I don't have that," he explains. "Plus, it's not like I can just walk into a fancy restaurant and ask the head chef to give me lessons. I have to teach myself. But you . . . you're more—"

"Blackmail-able?" I ask, crossing my arms.

"Accessible," he says, smiling and shaking his head. "And impossible."

I take a deep breath. I can admit that this probably isn't the worst thing in the world for Justin to ask of me, and the longer I take to agree, the more time I could give him to come up with more demands . . . But there's still a problem.

"We can't use store equipment for personal pizza lessons," I say, no snark or sarcasm.

"You could come to my house," he offers, not missing a beat.

Because that went so well last time, I think to myself.

"I'll buy all the supplies," he goes on. "We have a big kitchen that barely gets used. All you'd have to do is show up and try not to be so . . . so—"

"So *what*?" I ask. I put my hands on my hips and cock my head to the side for show, which makes Justin laugh.

"Just be patient with me," he says finally.

My pocket vibrates, so I pull out my phone. Mom texted *All good?* which is usually what comes before *What's taking so long?*

I feel like my dad when he knows he's about to lose a neighborhood basketball game. No more overtime. No more moves to pull. Just the fact of the loss.

"I guess I can manage that," I relent.

"Deal," Justin says.

I shake his outstretched hand before we turn and head back into Soul Slice.

chapter 8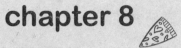

At lunch the next day, I'm on my way to meet Devin in the art room when I stop and take my time looking around the art hallway.

I see the treehouse sculpture again, and the weaving beside the loom. The walls are covered in student art, far more colorful and imaginative than what hung on the walls at my old school. Our arts program was underfunded, too, but like *city* underfunded, not suburb "underfunded." We didn't have a kiln or a ceramics program. We didn't always have acrylic paint, and sometimes we'd have to spend the whole semester using watercolor paint that Mrs. Plume bought from the dollar store with her own money. We made do, and Brooklyn itself is a piece of art. There are studios and art camps and weekend programs that my parents sent me to when they could. But now I can't help but wonder how much better of an artist I might be if I grew up here in Hempstead.

Here, if you want to do an oil painting, you don't have to worry that there won't be enough supplies. If you want to do a coil sculpture or one of those Greek vases from the Disney *Hercules* movie, you just have to ask for more clay.

I study the sculptures inside the display case, most of them abstract. One that catches my eye is an abstract tree. When Mr. Chris steps out of the classroom and sees me looking at the tree sculpture, he tells me that one of his students from a few years ago made the piece after her dad died. For a while, she didn't want to do any work. She stopped creating altogether. But for her final project, she went into the school's courtyard and started collecting sticks. She used twine to make the tree—one thick textured stick for the trunk and a bunch of smaller twigs tied to it with the twine. All the chaos was connected to the central object by a single string. All her feelings were coming out of her every which way, but they were part of her, tied to her.

That's deep! That's the kind of thing that wins an art festival/competition. As I follow Mr. Chris into the classroom, I worry that my boxy replica of Soul Slice won't cut it. Maybe it needs something else, something more than appliances and furniture.

But I don't have any ideas even once I'm working in the art room alongside Devin.

On the walk to Soul Slice that afternoon with Justin, I'm quiet, still thinking about my project.

"Are you okay?" Justin asks, holding the door open for me.

"Yeah," I say, sighing.

Justin follows me to the delivery station, and I punch in my code and scout my next few deliveries.

"You seem kind of far away," he says.

I start pulling orders out of the convection oven, and Justin holds the delivery bag open for me, zipping it shut when I finish.

"I'm just thinking about stuff," I admit.

Justin goes to say hi to his dad, who's in the office with my parents.

"What are they up to?" I ask Justin when he returns.

"Your parents can't decide on what furniture they want to use. They managed to pick out some light fixtures, and my dad said that a crew will come tomorrow to seal the holes in the ceiling and start painting since the electrician finished today."

"In other words, boring stuff," I say, teasing.

"You should show your parents the drawings for your project," Justin says, his tone serious.

"No."

"Why not? Your ideas are really good and I'm sure they could find something online that comes close to your designs."

"Justin, they are *my* ideas. My art is the one thing that is truly mine right now, and I don't want it getting hijacked as another part of the move and grand opening. Please drop this."

Justin throws his hands up in surrender and starts backing away. But before he can disappear, he adds, "All I'm saying is that if you helped out, this whole thing would go by a lot faster and maybe they'd be able to open and hire more drivers and you could go to art club without it having to be a secret."

"*Or,*" I say, shouldering my delivery bag and moving past him, "you could mind your business."

o ❤ o ❤ o

My shift goes by pretty fast. By the time the sun is setting, there are no more deliveries left for me, so I start restocking the salad station. Justin gets permission from his dad to hang with me, which turns out to involve hovering in my personal space while I try to work.

"Hey, Dad? " Justin asks when our parents come out of the office.

"Yeah, kid?"

"Can we order a pizza for dinner?"

Justin's dad looks at my parents, and my dad tells him it's on the house. Dad grabs a nearby apron, asking Justin what he wants on his pizza.

Pepperoncini instead of pepperoni, I think to myself, smiling.

"Actually, do you think Maya could make it? And can I watch?"

Suddenly I go from being crouched on the floor in front of the salad station with a bucket of lettuce in my hands—aka blissfully invisible—to having all eyes on me.

"If Maya is okay with it?" Mom says, and I shrug, which everyone takes as a yes.

Dad hands me the apron, and I have to tie it so that the middle is folded enough that the hem doesn't touch the floor. For fun, my mom gets Justin an apron, too, and we head to the topping line to where we keep the pre-panned dough. I explain how we make dough in the morning and there's a fridge where we store it. Then we bring it out and stretch it to fit different-size pans for the different-size pizzas. When I ask Justin if he wants a large, since it's on the house, he admits that it'll just be him and his dad eating it, so they might as well go with a medium.

We work around the crew members stationed at the topping line, waiting until the ladle for sauce is free. It's funny, watching Justin's expressions go from curious to intently listening to looks of wonder and excitement.

"So cool," he says.

"You're acting like pizza making is a whole journey," I tell him, reaching for a handful of mushrooms.

"It is, in a way," he says, pointing to the container of tomatoes. "How do you know how much of each topping to put on? And how do you spread it so evenly?"

You just do is the immediate answer that comes to mind, but I know that's not helpful. As I evenly distribute the tomato chunks over his custom masterpiece, I try to think back to when I was little and my parents taught me how to make pizza. You sprinkle the toppings, moving your hand in a circle and letting go of a consistent amount. The circular motion of your hand grows based on the size of the pizza. The amount you grab is also based on this.

I explain it to Justin, knowing that it doesn't really do it justice.

"I feel like you'll get it when you do it yourself," I say.

"Right. Saturday, then," he says.

"Do you have all the supplies?" I ask, flicking my wrist for some flair when I add the layer of Parmesan cheese to the top.

"I think so, but I'll check tonight," he says, distracted. "So, what now?"

"We cook it," I say, handing him the pan.

We go over to the mouth of the oven. The back and front are both open, and there's a metal belt that carries the pizza through at a slow enough pace that it cooks all the way by the time it comes out the other side. I like it because it's efficient. Instead of setting a few pizzas in the oven and waiting for them to be done, the oven itself is on a loop and you just keep adding to it.

"Be careful," I murmur, watching as Justin lifts the pan and sets it on the belt.

Slowly, the oven swallows it, and we have nothing left to do but wait.

"This is awesome," Justin says after a moment of watching the pizza.

"I guess."

I can't deny that I feel a tiny bit excited for Justin to taste the pizza . . . because I made it.

"I hope you like it," I say, pulling my apron off.

"Do you want to try it?" he asks, catching me off guard. "You could come over for dinner."

"Oh, I—uh—I still have to work. I don't think my shift is over."

"It is," Mom says, rounding the corner from the delivery station. "Have dinner with your friend, honey. It's been a little busy tonight, so your dad and I won't be home until later anyways. Just try to get some homework done." She says the last part more to Mr. Avery than to me, parent to parent.

Homework and dinner aside, I don't want to go to Justin's house before I absolutely have to. He has me a little stressed. Our "deal" is another part of the lie I'm keeping up in front of my parents—a lie that I don't want to get caught in for too many reasons.

Plus, I'm kidding myself. Justin and I are only hanging out because of our parents and the decision to use each other for personal gain—an odd but surprisingly effective combination. In an alternate universe, our paths wouldn't cross outside school. We're not friends. He's popular. I mean, he's always with Waverly or with his guy friends. I even overheard him and his friends talking about how they can't wait for basketball to start at the end of October and how he spent half his summer in North Carolina at a baseball camp, using his free time to chill on the beach. I spent my summer running around in denial.

"I actually have a lot of work to do on my art project, and—well, you know—I don't get much time during the week," I say, feeling a little shy since what I'm saying is mostly honest but still covering up the truth.

"All right," Justin says. "Then I guess I'll just see you Saturday."

chapter 9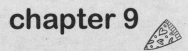

"OMG, so this is, like, your first date?" Sasha asks that night, leaning in so close to her phone that her smile nearly takes up my entire screen.

"Dude, back up," I say, laughing. "And this is *not* a date. Not even in the slightest. Did you hear me when I explained the whole *I'm using him, he's using me* part?"

"It sounds like he basically finessed you into spending time with him," Sasha reasons, raising her eyebrows.

"He wasn't trying to spend more time with me," I correct her, pulling photos out of one of the last cardboard boxes in my room. "He just wants to learn how to make pizza."

"While spending time with you," Sasha adds,

nodding dramatically to push her point.

I roll my eyes, knowing there's no winning with her.

I look through the pictures, sorting them rapidly into piles. There's Sasha and me, family pictures, pictures from school trips and vacations. These photos used to frame my closet mirror in our old house, so I'll have to figure out a way to stick them to the mirror on the back of my door here.

"How's the art cloob?" Sasha asks, pronouncing *club* like *cube* with an *l*.

"The cloob was cool," I say. "It's great to get to do *something* not pizza related."

"For a pizza-related price," she says, laughing.

"UGH, I can't wait until this grand opening is over with," I say through a yawn. "How are things over there?" I ask.

"Well, since you asked," she says in a singsong voice. "I actually have some news."

"Ooooh, what is it?"

"Well, I found a date to the Snowflake dance."

A ton of questions and feelings flood me at once. "Who? When? How? And *already*?"

The Snowflake dance happens every November. I imagine that it's like a mini version of what prom will be like. There're always sparkly winter-themed decorations, and it's the one event where everyone really gets dressed up. The parents who plan it even have fancy finger food catered instead of setting out the usual cheese and vegetable platters.

"I know, like, it kind of just *happened*," Sasha admits, adjusting her silk cap and leaning back in bed. "Jeffrey Doman actually asked me."

I climb into my bed, making a comforter tent over my knees and around the back of my head, the light from my phone keeping my face from disappearing into total darkness.

"That's great," I say, a smile plastered to my face.

"Yeah, it was pretty low-key. He came to my locker after school and had a flower—and it was obvious he picked it from the garden by the front office, but still. It was just cute, you know? And nice. I honestly wasn't even sure if I'd find a date, and now I've found one, like, months in advance."

I'm happy for her, but as she continues gushing

details, I realize that I might be a little jealous. I move to Pennsylvania, and suddenly one of the cutest guys in our grade asks Sasha to the dance.

"Is he just a date, or do you think it's something more?" I ask.

"I'm not sure yet. This happened today. We exchanged numbers, so I figure I'll wait and see if he texts me at all this weekend."

"You'll have to keep me posted," I say, feeling a wave of homesickness.

There's a part of me that wishes I was there. Maybe Jeffrey has a friend that would've asked me and we would be plotting a double date right now, having a sleepover where we keep our phones in front of us faceup all night while rewatching the *To All the Boys I've Loved Before* trilogy on Netflix.

"Do you know if Hempstead has any dances?" Sasha asks.

The question pulls me out of my make-believe movie night and back into the real world. "I have no idea, to be honest," I say. "Not that there's anyone who would want to go with me."

"I bet Justin would go with you," she says suggestively, wagging her brows up and down.

I blush at the thought but quickly push it away. "I don't think I'm his type."

"How could you possibly know that when you keep him at arm's length?"

"Because he and this girl Waverly are, like, a thing."

Sasha scrunches up her face. "I thought you said they were distinctly *not* a thing, that Waverly just wanted to be."

"Yeah, but it's not like he's told her no," I say.

"That is a tricky one, I guess," she admits, taking her turn to yawn.

We fall silent for a moment, and I can feel my eyes getting heavy.

"Maybe you can ask him about it."

I must have dreamt that she said that. I open my eyes wide and blink myself awake. "What did you say?"

"Why don't you just ask him about it at your pizza lesson?"

"Maybe because that would be plain weird. Like, if I ask him about it, he might think I care," I say, incredulous that she would make that suggestion in the first place. "Next thing I know, he'll tell Waverly, and after they have a good laugh, it'll be all over school that I have a crush on him."

"Which you don't . . ." Sasha says, though it comes out sounding more like a question.

"Correct," I affirm, staring into her eyes on my screen.

"Okay," she says, shrugging her shoulders. "It's up to you. You'll never know unless you ask, so I guess you don't really want to know."

That's something my MaMa would say. If I asked for ice cream but wasn't willing to spend my own allowance, she would say I must not really want the ice cream. It would drive me crazy. It's driving me crazy right now.

The fact that half our FaceTime conversation has been taken over by Justin is driving me crazy!

When Sasha yawns again and it proves to be contagious, we decide to say good night. The chime that sounds the end of our call has come to signify my window to home closing. I lie there, letting my comforter collapse onto me, and stay in the darkness for a little while. I pretend that outside my makeshift tent is my old room, and beyond that is my old life.

I hate this feeling, knowing that there's so much going on without me. And I know it's selfish because I have so much going on here, and it's not like I can ask Sasha to stop her life.

Still under my blanket, I roll over and start trying to make myself into a burrito. When I hear something hit the floor, I free myself, pulling the cover down and surfacing in my real room—not the old room that felt so real in my imagination. I lean over the foot of my bed and see that I kicked off some of my schoolbooks. I gather them and find a piece of torn notebook paper left behind on the carpet.

When I flip it over, I instantly know what it is.

In the sloppy handwriting that I always accidentally glance at during English class since it's, like, *right there*, there's a note:

Sorry about yesterday. Hope you can forgive me.

At least you know how to make a band-aid look good. ☺

I was in such a hurry to get out of class that first day of school that I never read Justin's note.

Reflexively, I reach up and touch my chin. I put on a fresh Band-Aid after my shower, as I've been doing every day since the disaster. The cut is just barely beginning to scab . . . because it's so new. So much has happened since that day.

Sasha is right. How could I possibly know Justin when we *just* met and I've been keeping him at arm's length? Every assumption that I've made so far has been wrong, so maybe I should stop assuming and get to know him for who he actually is.

chapter 10

In the spirit of turning over a new leaf, I decide to bring some of my own supplies to our pizza-making lesson on Saturday. Before Dad leaves to open the shop, I convince him to make a few extra dough balls for me to use as our pizza bases. That way Justin and I won't have to waste time waiting for the dough to rise. I also bring some leftover chicken breast and Mom's homemade BBQ sauce—the same one she uses on Soul Slice pizzas.

The rack on the back of my bike turns out to be pretty handy for carrying everything, and I follow my GPS to get to Justin's house. This time, the house doesn't seem ominous. It just looks and feels plain. Not good, not bad, not homey, but plain.

The doorbell chime doesn't even finish before Justin pulls open the front door and welcomes me inside.

"Aww, you brought presents," he coos, placing a hand over his heart.

"You would like that, wouldn't you," I say, shoving him on our way to the kitchen.

Once you step out of the foyer, his house opens up. The living room is bathed in light from a bay window framed with cerulean curtains. Past the living room, toward the back of the house, is an elaborate dining room with a dark wood table and matching chairs, overseen by a stained-glass chandelier. Directly ahead of us is the kitchen, with a glass sliding door onto the back patio.

There's so much light and warmth. There are tribal sculptures and masks placed in such a way that they pull your eyes from room to room on a scavenger hunt. Standing at the threshold of the kitchen is a black sculpture of a baby with carved curls and a basket on top of its head.

"My mom picked most of the art for the house," Justin says when he catches me staring.

"This is the kind of stuff my grandma collects," I admit. "Is your mom a designer, too?"

"She is," Justin says.

Now that I'm thinking about it, I realize I haven't heard anything about Justin's mom, nor have I seen her.

"What's she like?" I ask, feeling nosy.

"She's like any other mom," he says, looking down instead of at me.

"If there's one thing I've learned, it's that no two moms are the same," I tell him as we step into the kitchen.

"She travels a lot for work," he says, though it comes out in a mumble. I get the vibe that he doesn't want to say more, so I drop it, not wanting to ruin what's shaping up to be a decent day.

"Where's your dad?" I ask, all the open space making me realize how alone we are.

The kitchen is a masterpiece. Stainless-steel appliances, a six-burner stove, a blue tile backsplash and white cabinets. There are two ovens in the wall and two dishwashers.

"On a walk. He'll be back soon," Justin says, falling a few steps behind me.

"How many people live here?" I ask, though I have a feeling about the answer.

"Just me, my dad, and my mom."

"Why all the . . . amenities?" I ask, setting my bag on the island, where Justin has already laid out various ingredients, pans, bowls, and chopped toppings.

"Honestly, I didn't pick the house," Justin says, laughing a little. It's clipped, though, and I can hear something else through it.

"Do you like it?" I ask, climbing onto one of the bar stools.

"What do you mean?" he asks, though I feel like he knows.

"Do you wish it was smaller?"

He considers this, cupping the back of his head with his hand and turning to look at the kitchen in its entirety.

"Sometimes," he says, no laughter or kidding in his voice.

Sensing his sincerity, I remember what Mikayla said about the personal details he shared with Waverly. I wonder if any of them were true.

"Are you afraid of four-leaf clovers?" I ask.

This makes him smile. "Seriously?"

"Answer the question," I say, snatching a piece of chopped bell pepper from one of the toppings bowls.

"Do you *think* I'm afraid of four-leaf clovers?" he asks, eyebrows raised.

Smiling, I say, "You never know." Moving on from that, I ask, "Do you have a dog?"

Justin squints at me, a knowing smile slipping across his lips. "On a walk with my dad."

I nod, and he nods, too, waiting for my next move.

"What's going on?" he asks, leaning against the counter and crossing his arms.

"Tell me something about you," I say, crossing my arms to mimic him. "Something that no one knows."

"What makes you think you deserve that?"

"I don't," I say, not missing a beat. "I just want to know."

"You first," he says.

We stare each other down while I think. *Something cool. Something interesting. Something that won't get me embarrassed but doesn't seem like I'm trying too hard.*

"I want to go to France and try snails," I say, feeling fairly confident but hoping he doesn't decide I'm gross.

"There's no way that *no one* knows that."

"Actually, no one does. My mom is from Italy, and my parents' dream is to save up and visit family there. I figured I'd be kind of a disappointment to say, 'Oh, instead of visiting relatives and learning more about half of my heritage, I'd rather go somewhere else entirely so I can chew on a slug,'" I say, relieved when Justin starts laughing.

"You have your own dreams—a little unconventional, but your own nonetheless. Nothing about that should be disappointing."

I feel kind of flighty, like—even though I'm standing here—gravity doesn't apply to my organs. It's a weird but good feeling.

"Your turn," I say, getting up and starting to unload my tote of supplies.

Justin watches while drumming his fingers on the counter, thinking about his answer.

"Okay, if you ever repeat this, I will deny it," he warns. "But I want to be a chef."

"Why is that a secret?" I ask, grabbing the paper towels off the counter to wipe it down. Once it's clean, I douse an empty space on the island with flour before handing Justin his dough ball.

"Because if anyone knew, it might somehow get back to my parents," Justin replies. "You're not the only one afraid of being a disappointment." He says it jokingly, but there's still truth to it.

"Why would you being a chef be a disappointment?"

"Both of my parents work in design. My dad does interior design, and my mom does architecture. I have no artistic skill whatsoever, but I haven't told them yet."

I guess I haven't given it much thought before, but I realize I haven't exactly been jumping at the chance to one day take over Soul Slice from my parents. I can cook. They taught me all the recipes, and I know how to make them at home from scratch if I ever want to . . . which I never do. Mom and Dad have always been pretty supportive of my art, but now in Hempstead, this is the first time that their dream—Soul Slice—has intersected with mine—attending art club.

This is also the first time that I've been forced into the reality where their dream *trumps* mine.

"What do you like to cook?" I ask, not wanting to go deeper into that line of thought as long as I can help it.

Justin follows my lead as I start to knead the dough. For me, the motion is mindless, as natural as riding my bike. Dig knuckles down into a pillow of chilled softness, then press the heel of my hand into it, pull back from the far end, and repeat. I fall back into the motion instantly, and for some reason, this reminds me how long it's been since I've kneaded dough.

"Anything, really," he admits. "I like following recipes and then adding to them as I go along. I also like learning new things, like the process of making pizza, for example."

He smiles, finding his rhythm.

"Well, you start by making the dough, but since we already have it premade, we get to skip that step. Next, we knead it into a ball. You can either roll it out or use your knuckles to kind of loosen it and spread it into a circle—"

"Is that where you throw it up in the air?" he asks, his tone giving away how badly he wants to do that.

"I guess, but I don't do it that way."

I show him how I start pressing the ball with my hands to flatten it. Then I pick it up and rest it on top of my closed fists, letting my knuckles dig in and work it apart. I spread out the center and then widen my hands and keep spreading the dough evenly until I have a circle that's the right amount of thick to make a cushiony crust.

We spray trays with oil and lay our crusts down. What follows is, in my opinion, the best part. The dough is usually all the same, but making different pizzas with different flavors and toppings and ratios of sauce to cheese is where each one comes into its own as something unique and individual.

We set to work replicating the BBQ chicken pizza from our menu. We have authentic Soul Slice dough, the homemade sauce, and some juicy leftover chicken breast—I personally think leftovers always taste a little better because they have time to rest.

We get so caught up—using a ladle to spread the sauce evenly, and me explaining how to twirl your wrist to get a perfect circle when drizzling your toppings—that when the pizzas go into the oven, our conversation comes to a halt. Both of us set to work cleaning up in the silence, the running water from the sink the only noise echoing in the largely empty space. It seems like the more noise we make, the bigger the house feels.

"So, I have a thought," Justin says, closing the dirty dishes inside the dishwasher.

"How rare," I tease. "Go on."

"BBQ chicken is great, and I know that your sauce is what makes it original," he says, his tone leading. He's looking at the counter, his eyes going back and forth like he's doing math in his head or something. "But," he continues, looking at me, "what if you took it a step further and made a BBQ rib pizza? And you could add toppings inspired by a backyard barbecue."

The moment it comes out of his mouth, I can already picture a pie with shredded rib meat; a thicker, smokier sauce; and toppings like grilled bell peppers and onions, maybe even some pineapple.

"Justin, that sounds amazing," I gush. "You have to run that by my parents. I'm sure they'd love it."

"Really?" he asks. His smile is so big that it pinches his cheeks into two clementines.

"Yes, really," I say, already imagining how excited my parents will be, especially if they decide to release it as a new pizza in time for the opening.

"On one condition," Justin says.

"Not another one of these," I say, moaning.

"Relax. You just have to share your design ideas with my dad, and then I'll share my pizza ideas with your parents."

"Please tell me you're joking."

"I promise, I'm not."

I don't really have to think this one through. As much as I want to keep my art separate from Soul Slice, Justin's idea really does sound like a hit, and I know what it would mean to my parents.

"Deal," I say, holding out my hand.

Justin swats my hand away. "No, this one we gotta dab up."

I shake my head, chuckling. Of course, that's what I should've expected. He is a wannabe G after all.

The garage door opens, and the empty quietness of the house is filled with the clatter of doggy nails tapping the tile, huffing and puffing, and loud barks. A full-grown chocolate Lab clambers up to Justin, standing on her hind legs to reach up to his chest. She then notices me sitting at the island and races to my stool, trying and failing to jump into my lap. Her claws press into my legs, forcing me to stand up so gravity won't work against me.

"Cher, come here, girl," Justin's dad says from the kitchen entrance. She obeys, running over to him. "Hi, Maya. How are you?"

"I'm good. How are you?"

"Good, good. I take it the pizza making is going well. The house smells amazing."

Justin brings his dad up to speed on the BBQ pizza while I pet Cher. Mr. Avery excuses himself to shower so he can get comfortable in time to enjoy a slice of our pizza.

When he's gone, I turn to Justin and ask, "What do you see in Waverly?"

His eyes get wide, and his brows scrunch together—he's clearly caught off guard. I feel nervous, but then I remind myself that I don't care. This isn't about me liking him so much as it's about me genuinely wanting to know. Especially now that I've seen more of the real Justin—who isn't rude, who has a secret passion, and who is actually pretty easy to talk to. I just want to know what a guy as nice and smart as him is doing almost with a girl as basic as Waverly.

He scratches his brow, looking down at the jar of BBQ sauce still open on the counter. "She's cool." His tone is noncommittal.

"Care to elaborate?" I ask, feeling bold since he's been so open.

"Care to tell me what the secret ingredient is in the sauce?" he asks, mocking my tone and holding up the BBQ bottle so that the label is facing me—advertising that the ingredients label tells you everything except for that special *something*. There's a drawing of a woman in an apron on the front, meant to be a younger rendition of MaMa, winking.

"If I told you, that would defeat the whole point," I say, taking the bottle and twisting on the cap.

I decide not to press, figuring if Justin doesn't want to share, then maybe I don't want to know.

chapter 11

On Monday after school, I wait for Justin at the bike rack. When I see him walk out the side door, I get a little excited. I was thinking that maybe for our next pizza lesson we could tackle the Biscuits and Gravy since that was his favorite from art club. Or, if we can gather all the ingredients, we could try making the BBQ rib pizza.

But then Waverly and a couple more kids come out behind him, all of them laughing together and passing around a basketball.

I begin to worry that they're going to walk with us, but then the guys fall back and Waverly and Justin stop together in front of a black Volkswagen. The way Waverly laughs and runs her hands through her straight hair makes me feel small. I'd never be able to comb my fingers clean through my nappy curls; they'd get caught or make a knot. My box braids even get tangled sometimes.

Waverly has on cat eyeliner that makes her eyes seem friendly, like a girl you'd want to talk to just to get to know. Her outfits never fail to look put together: tank tops with tasteful crew necks, miniskirts, and an array of strappy sandals and chic ballerina flats. She's not trying too hard, but at the same time simple does so much. Meanwhile, I wear boxy homemade T-shirts and jeans. I like my style, don't get me wrong, but maybe it could be doing more for me—like make me feel cute . . . or something.

Clearly, I'm not the cute one. I'm not the one Justin is leaning in to hug. I'm not the one Jeffrey Doman asked to the Snowflake dance—and did, it turns out, text Sasha over the weekend. I'm just the pizza delivery girl.

"Hey," Justin says when he closes the distance between us.

Waverly's car pulls off, and she waves to Justin

through her rolled-down window before turning the corner and disappearing in the direction we are about to head.

"Hi," I say, trying to shake off my nerves as we fall in step beside each other.

"Good day?"

"Yeah," I say, pretending to focus on steering my bike over the cracks in the sidewalk. "You?"

"I got a B on my history quiz," he says.

"Cool, congrats," I say, instantly feeling awkward and weird. We don't do small talk. We never do small talk. We either insult each other or we just regular talk.

I worry that something's changed, that I made things weird by asking too many personal questions on Saturday. Or maybe Sasha was wrong, and asking about Waverly *has* led him to believe that I have a crush on him, and now he's being standoffish because he doesn't know how to go about "letting me down easy."

There's no way he would ask me to the Snowflake dance.

"Listen," Justin says, pulling me out of my avalanche of thoughts. I glance up at him and he's looking at me, something intense in his eyes. "I was thinking—"

"Something you don't do often," I say, teasing.

Justin laughs a little but gets serious again. "I was thinking about our deal, and I don't think pizza making is enough."

Trying to keep an open mind, I entertain him. "So, what else do you want?"

"I want to run more deliveries with you. Well, at least today."

"That was a one-time thing," I remind him, trying not to sound snarky. "Plus, I'm faster on my bike."

"I can walk fast. I just need you to make sure that I take deliveries with you *today*," he insists.

"Justin, I'm sorry, but no. That'll interfere with my work," I say, hoping he's not offended.

"Don't you even want to know why?"

"Not really," I say, feeling a little annoyed that he can't just respect my answer. "It won't change the fact that I'm *faster on my bike* than on foot."

"Don't make me do this," he says, shaking his head.

"Do *what*?"

"Pull the art club card," he says.

"Excuse me?" That did *not* just come out of his mouth.

"If you don't get my dad to let me take deliveries with you today, I'll tell your parents about art club."

"You're the WORST!" I shout loud enough that the kids walking ahead of us turn around.

"Maya, come on. Please?"

"*Please?* You just threatened me. Don't act like I have a choice if you're not going to give me one. That's so messed up."

"Hey, whatever it takes," he says, shrugging like this is somehow out of his hands.

Whatever it takes? What the heck!

I speed up and walk ahead of him. It was cute when Justin just wanted to learn how to make pizza. This, however, is taking it too far. This is not fun. It's not cute. It's, like, *actual* blackmail.

I fume the whole way to Soul Slice. I'm not willing to give up art club, though, so before we pass in front of the shopwindow, I stop. I tilt my bike and lift up my foot, bringing it down as hard as I can on the chain. I stomp it and kick it hard enough that the pressure makes it snap, the links scattering across the sidewalk.

My parents decided that we would move. My parents decided I had to help out with the opening. *I* decided to find a way to do art. It was the one thing that I got to pick for myself out of all this mess, but now Justin has decided to dangle that over my head.

"Maya, wait! Stop—"

"This is what you wanted," I say, glaring at Justin. "Right? I can't make deliveries alone if I don't have a bike."

I refocus my attention, nearly tripping over a piece of the chain when I try to move my bike closer to the wall, but Justin runs up and puts his hand on my arm. I instantly shove him away.

"Never touch me again!"

Justin throws his hands up in surrender. I pick up my bike and lean it against the shop. Instead of letting him get the door for me, I yank it open.

I hear a loud noise over my head and worry that the ceiling is finally giving out. When I jump back, Justin's dad comes over—wearing a hard hat.

"We got a bell for the door. That way when

customers come in, everyone will be able to hear," he tells me with a smile. "What do you think?"

Instead of stating the obvious—that it's loud and annoying—I say, "It works." I glance behind me at Justin and his blackmailing face. "Do you think Justin can help me with deliveries today? My bike chain broke, and there's no way I'll be able to carry the deliveries by myself."

"Oh, of course. Yeah, he can help out," his dad says, all smiles.

Right then, I decide that I'm no longer speaking to Justin because it seems like the more I do that, the harder my life gets. Within minutes, I'm clocked in, our stuff is in the cabinet, and we are out the door with an order of five small pizzas.

What's worse is that we have to go up McGregor Street to get to the address, and that's where the most unbelievably steep hill is.

"Are you really not going to talk to me?" Justin asks for the fifth time.

It's going to be a long day if he keeps this up, but I figure I'm not the one wasting my breath.

"Really?" he says.

Yes, really.

I can't wait to tell Sasha she was more than wrong about Justin. And I can't wait for her to finally be on my side and see how much of a jerk he is.

We hike up McGregor hill, Justin huffing and puffing behind me. I no longer have to wonder if it's harder to get up on a bike or on foot. I know from firsthand experience that it's WAY HARDER ON FOOT. Plus, I won't get the satisfaction of flying downhill on the way back, taking my feet off the pedals and letting the breeze dry the sweat on my skin. Justin stole that from me, too.

"It should be three houses down on the right," Justin says behind me.

I stop to check the GPS, and he's right. Then I realize that he never saw the address, not on the monitor or the ticket that's in my pocket.

I follow him up a walkway lined with tiny hedges, fragrant with fresh mulch. The front door is white with a silver knocker, but Justin rings the doorbell and stands back. He takes a second to pull his chain out of his shirt so that it falls just below his collar. He turns the Soul Slice employee cap that my parents gave him—since he's an honorary employee for the day—around so that it's backward. If I was talking to him, I'd tell him he's pathetic.

Justin leans in again, this time using the knocker. Laughter comes from inside the house, and I can hear someone, a girl, telling us that she's coming.

Next thing I know, Waverly is pulling open the front door and leaning against the frame.

"Hey, you," she says, her eyes glued to Justin.

"What's good?" Justin asks, smiling.

Waverly notices me standing behind him and her smile falls like ten stories underground. "You brought *her*?"

Before I can correct her and inform her that *I* actually brought *him* on *my* delivery, she's interrupted by a couple of boys howling like wolves behind her. The two guys that followed them out of school earlier materialize. One guy stands by the door, gesturing for us to come inside. I've seen him in the hallways at school, usually across the cafeteria at Justin and

Waverly's table. Justin dabs him up and I follow behind, surprised when the boy takes my delivery bag off my shoulder.

"Thanks," I say as he closes the door behind me.

"No problem. I'm David."

"Maya," I say.

"Like Maya Angelou?"

"Actually, yeah." My dad loves her poetry, but most people don't make the connection between our names.

"That's cool," David says, smiling.

"I take it this is your house?"

Before he can answer, a woman comes to the top of the stairs, asking who was at the door.

"This is Maya. She and Justin just got here with the pizza."

"Hello, hon." The woman smiles, her freckles and dark brown hair resembling David enough that it answers my question.

"Hi," I say, feeling a little shy.

"Help yourselves. There are Popsicles in the freezer and soda in the fridge. I'll be up here."

She disappears back down the hallway, and David

leads me farther into the house. We head to the kitchen, where Justin already left behind his delivery bag on the table.

David sets my bag down next to Justin's, asking, "Can I get you something to drink?"

As nice as that would be, I'm focused on making good time getting back to the shop. "We actually can't stay long," I tell him.

"Oh. Doesn't that defeat the purpose of coming to study group, if you can't stay for study group?" he asks, pulling a couple of plastic cups out of a bag on the counter.

"Study group?"

Outside I hear a splash and a scream. Looking out the kitchen window, I see Waverly sitting next to Justin on the edge of a pool at the bottom of a set of stone steps. Their friend, the howler, surfaces in the deep end with a water gun aimed at them.

"Are you having a pool party?" I ask.

David holds out a cup of soda, and I accept, savoring the chilled condensation already sweating on the side of the cup.

"Justin didn't tell you?"

Actually, no, he failed to mention that he was using me to come hang out with his friends.

"No," I say, feeling a bunch of things at once. Annoyed. Angry. Used. Hurt because I was used. Betrayed. Nervous.

Maybe a little bit curious about David and his dimples, but mostly those other feelings.

"Wanna help me set up?" David asks, unzipping the bag closest to him.

I figure helping him—the customer—counts as work, so I unzip the delivery bag in front of me and pull out three small pizzas. When I note the two David has in his hands, I realize that there's one for each of us—Justin, David, Waverly, Water Gun Guy, and me. Justin planned this. He *planned* to use me.

David grabs plates and napkins, and I follow him outside onto the back patio. We make our way down the cobblestone steps, past a man-made koi pond, and over to a table by the pool. Once he sets everything down, David pulls out his phone, and within seconds, music thunders from speakers hidden in the backyard.

Travis Scott's low rumbling voice drones on about goose bumps, and Justin and I reflexively make eye contact. Between two white dudes and a Korean girl, this is not what I would've expected to be at the top of the playlist.

However, I must admit that being here takes me back to summer afternoons at the community pool in New York. When Sasha and I were little, Mom would let one of the older boys from the neighborhood named Marcus, who played basketball with Dad, walk us to the pool since his mom made him take his little sister. He'd bring his Bluetooth speaker and snag a spot under one of the few trees near the deep end. One time, I asked Marcus why the people in his music talked and shouted instead of singing. He was the first person to ever tell me to listen closer to the words than to the beat of the songs, and just like that, rap made so much sense to me.

David runs, jumps, and cannonballs into the pool, water splashing up over the edge and sprinkling onto my skin.

Standing by myself in this random backyard, I feel

simultaneously invisible and exposed. I pull out my phone and text Devin:

> *JUSTIN TRICKED ME INTO LETTING HIM HELP WITH DELIVERIES. NOW I'M AT A POOL PARTY WITH YOUR SISTER!*

Within seconds, she replies: *OMG WHAT THE HECK!*

"Maya Angelou, are you okay?" David asks, crossing the patio, leaving footprints on the concrete now that he's dripping wet.

"Yeah, I think the heat's just getting to me a little," I say, not wanting to reveal the truth, which is that I've never been to a pool party with boys before. I'm not even sure if I'm allowed to be at a pool party with boys.

I mean, technically I'm not allowed to be at a pool party at all right now since I'm on the clock.

"If you're hot, you could take a dip and cool off," he suggests, an amused look brightening his face.

Right, because this is a pool party.

"No bathing suit," I say, shrugging and trying to make myself sound disappointed.

"You could sit on the edge, get your feet wet and rate Carter's and my cannonballs," he suggests.

On any other day, in an alternate universe where I wasn't working, and then in the parallel universe to that where without Soul Slice throwing Justin and me together we'd still hang out and he'd bring me to his friend's house, I would totally be down. But that's not the world we live in. That's *so* far removed from the world we live in . . .

"Relax," David says.

I don't have a good poker face, which means he can definitely tell that I'm having a mini freak-out. But I'm thankful that he's trying at least. Justin, on the other hand, is incredibly cozy with Waverly—me, my job, and my efforts to not get in trouble with my parents are the furthest things from his mind right now. It's ridiculous that I let myself begin to think he might care about someone other than himself.

"Guys, I am starving," Carter says, hauling himself over the edge of the pool.

Waverly and Justin get up from their spot to come join us at the table.

"Well, Maya Angelou, what have you prepared for us today?"

"Maya Angelou? Man, that's not her name," Justin says, giving David a little stank eye.

"Chill, it's a nickname," David says, passing out paper plates.

"When did you have time to come up with a nickname?" Justin asks, his voice a little snappy all of a sudden.

I stop myself from asking, *When did you have time to come up with a plan to ruin my life?*

"Let it go," I say instead, opening the boxes.

It looks like there's two Fried Chicken and Waffle pizzas, one BBQ chicken, a Corn Bread Crust, and a Biscuits and Gravy.

"I thought I told you to get me pepperoni," Waverly whines.

"Pepperoni is so basic. Plus, the whole point of Soul Slice is their soul food pizzas," Justin explains, taking a slice of Biscuits and Gravy and a slice of Fried Chicken and Waffle—predictable.

"I don't like soul food," Waverly says. Even though

she's talking to Justin, she's looking at me when she says it. "It's greasy and gross."

"Well, the cheese is what usually makes it greasy," I tell her a little sharply. "So, you shouldn't worry about that. We tone down the cheese and play up the other flavors."

"Your loss," Carter says through a mouthful of BBQ chicken. "This slaps."

"Do you want some?" David asks me.

"Actually, Justin and I really need to get back to the shop," I say. Feeling my phone vibrating in my pocket, I slip it out just enough to take a peek. Mom is calling, but there's no way I can answer—not with this music blasting in the background.

"Maya—"

"No." Waverly cuts Justin off. "If she has to get back to work, let her."

Though I sense a little hostile, possibly jealous, energy, I admit, Waverly is onto something. Justin isn't actually a Soul Slice employee. Whether he's at the shop or not doesn't really matter, and—let's face it—I can handle carrying deliveries on foot for the rest of today. At least I won't have to be with *him*.

"Right," I say. I'm not wanted here. I don't belong here. So, why am I still standing around? "You guys have fun. I'm gonna go."

I head toward the gate leading to the driveway, lifting the latch and letting myself out. Already, on the other side of the wall, I feel some relief. Checking my phone, I see unread texts and two missed calls from Mom. If I make decent enough time, I might still be able to do some damage control—

"Maya, wait."

I keep walking.

"Stop, hold on."

Not a chance.

I reach the end of the driveway, but Justin steps in front of me. When he reaches out to me, I jerk back.

"You can't leave."

I widen my eyes and then proceed to show him that I can do just that by taking another step.

"If you leave, I'll tell your—"

"Shut UP! I hate you! I hate you! I hate you!" I shout, not caring who hears me.

"Maya—" he starts, his tone actually sounding hurt, like *he's* the victim here.

"Shut up! You suck," I say. Not my most impressive comeback, but it's still the truth.

For once, he listens.

I'm shaking. I don't know whether to be angry and kick the lamppost or to cry because of how frustrated I am.

"Do you really not see how messed up you're being right now?" I ask. "Art club is my One Good Thing about the move, the one thing that I have control over right now since the rest of my life is being decided by my parents and freaking pizza. No one asked me if I wanted to move. No one asked me if I wanted to help out at the shop. No one asked me how it would make me feel to leave my best friend behind. I was just supposed to roll with it, be supportive, and show up for my family. And yeah, I'm lying to my parents about art club, but it's not like I'm trying to go to some party after school and waste time. I'm trying to do something constructive, for myself. Like, you *really* went this far out of your way to hang out with Waverly, poolside?"

"I'm not here to hang out with Waverly," Justin says, because that's all he managed to take away from my rant.

I laugh. "Right, you were just willing to do *whatever it takes* to spend time with her at my expense."

His face falls, as if he hadn't realized that that's what he's doing.

"Look, I'm sorry. Okay?"

"No, you're not," I tell him. Maybe deep down he thinks he is, but I can see right through it. He's right where he wants to be.

"Just give me like two minutes to say bye to everyone, and then I'll walk back to Soul Slice with you," Justin promises.

And he does. I don't speak to him once the whole way.

By the time we make it back to Soul Slice, I'm so deep in my head trying to come up with believable excuses for why we're so late that I forget about the bell above the door. The chime startles me, making me cringe and taking away any chance of us sneaking inside unnoticed.

"Maya, where have you been!" Mom rushes over, taking me by the shoulders and giving me a once-over. Clearly, I'm unscathed, so her worry immediately transforms into fury. "What happened? We've been so worried about you. Why didn't you answer your phone?"

Before I have a chance to answer, Dad interjects and suggests we head to the office for some privacy. I look back at Justin, hoping and praying that he might dig me out of this hole. But he's just talking to his dad. I don't even matter.

With the door closed and my parents standing between me and any form of escape, I feel small.

"Where were you?" Mom asks again.

"My bike chain broke, and getting up the hill on foot took a lot longer than normal. I'm sorry," I say. "And the people wanted us to help them set up—"

"Set up? You went *into* their house?" she asks, her eyes practically falling out of her head.

"They were friends of Justin," I say. "They weren't strangers."

"Still, Maya, you never go into customers' houses.

You know that! What's gotten into you?" Her voice begins to rise. "You had us worried. We thought something might have happened to you. You weren't answering your phone! We aren't from here. We don't know our way around; we don't know the people here. What were you thinking?"

She's giving me *the look*. It's the look that gets me and my cousins to sit down and be quiet during family dinners. The look that gets employees to start showing up on time after Mom calls them out. It's the look that makes me feel smaller than a speck of sand.

With tears stinging the corners of my eyes, I grasp at straws. "I forgot to turn my phone volume on after school. I didn't hear it, Mom. I'm sorry. I'm so sorry."

"Maya, we are upset because we were scared. We love you, and we can't imagine what it would be like if anything happened to you," Dad says, crouching down in front of me.

"We gave you a phone so that you could talk *to us*," Mom says. "If you *ever* do something like this again, we will take your phone away. And you won't *get* to work anymore. You can be grounded at home. No phone, no

Sasha, and no art supplies. Do you understand?"

"Yes, ma'am," I say, though it comes out gurgly and congested. Tears rain down my face, and I nearly choke on the lump in my throat.

Mom leaves the office, closing the door behind her and leaving Dad and me alone. He pulls me in for a hug: bad cop, then good cop. I rest my head on his shoulder and wrap my arms around the back of his neck, feeling exhausted and hopeless.

"I'm sorry," I tell him, praying he believes me. "I didn't mean to make you worry."

"I know," he says, his voice soft. "I know."

chapter 12

That evening, after Dad helps me put a new chain on my bike, I text Devin a play-by-play of the day's events. It takes a lot of convincing to talk her down from barging into Waverly's room and giving her what she calls *the wrath*.

But Devin can't quite help herself. When we meet up before the bell at school the next day, she tells me how she poured orange juice into Waverly's almond milk that morning. Apparently, Waverly got as far as making her coffee and adding "milk" to her cereal, coming face-to-face with a spoonful of Cheerios swimming in something orange instead of white, before she realized. Apparently, the look was priceless. Apparently, it was so worth it that Devin isn't even salty she got her phone taken away for recording a video of the whole thing.

Even though it's nice to know Devin has my back, Waverly wasn't the issue yesterday. Justin is the one who acts nice one minute and rude the next. I still can't believe he once again took advantage of something that he knew was important to me.

In English class, I pointedly don't make eye contact with him, and when he slips me a note at the end of the period, I just leave it there. There's nothing he can say to fix this.

At lunchtime, Devin and I work on our projects in Mr. Chris's room. She's nearly finished sorting her collection of magazine cutouts by color and putting them into smaller Ziploc baggies that live inside the original big one. I've just been sitting here, having gotten as far as using thick poster board to make my walls and floor.

"Are you having artist's block?" Devin asks, chewing on a gummy worm.

"I guess. It feels like I'm missing something," I say, looking at my sketches.

"You have to put the soul in Soul Slice," Devin says, pausing her own work to look over mine.

"That's the cheesiest thing I've ever heard."

"That's definitely a lie, coming from the girl who's made a Mom's Mac 'n' Cheese pizza," Devin counters, giving me a knowing nod.

"Cheese aside," I say, not wanting to get off track. "What *is* the soul of Soul Slice?"

"Your family?"

Even though Devin is just tossing out the idea, she's spot-on. My family *and* the Soul Slice family of employees are what make the shop great. They make it unique. The soul food pizzas, the new color scheme, and the new employees—that's what's missing from my project.

"I need to go all out and add details," I say, the ideas flooding me. "It shouldn't just be a plain model showing where everything should go. The oven should *be* an oven. There should be mini pizza boxes stacked on the shelves, and tables with chairs in the seating area. And I need to make the employees, and my parents."

A smile takes over Devin's mouth, and her eyes light up. "I can totally see it."

Mr. Chris helps me brainstorm. Since I'm going all

out, we decide to scale the model bigger so that I don't get caught up trying to make everything so tiny. For the bulkier pieces—like walls and countertops—I can use poster board and paint it. For the smaller pieces, like the pizza oven, the topping line, and other appliances, I'll do research to see what miniature stuff—like dollhouse furniture—I can find online.

For the rest of the week, I throw myself into my project, working in the art room at lunch every day and in the evenings when I can. I'm thankful that Justin takes my hint and lays off. He doesn't try to apologize to me again or slip me any notes. At Soul Slice, he doesn't invite himself on any of my deliveries, and he doesn't even try to come with me to art club on Wednesday. He just hangs back at the shop, pretending to be interested in his dad's work. No mention of the BBQ rib pizza to my parents and no talk of my project to his dad.

By the end of the week, I realize Justin actually held up his end of our original deal. He kept my secret after all. Don't get me wrong, it was the *least* he could do.

So, on Saturday, I figure that—as a woman of

my word—I should keep up my end of the bargain. Though, by the surprised look on Justin's face when he opens his door to find me standing there with my bag of pizza supplies, I can tell we were both on the same page about me having every right to hate him and not show up today.

"You're here," he says as I move past him into the house.

"Keen observation," I mumble.

In the kitchen, I turn the oven on to preheat and start unloading my things, not wanting to waste time.

"I didn't think you would come," he admits, getting out the same tray we used last week.

I find the flour myself and douse the counter. Justin sits down across from me, probably noting that I brought only one dough ball this time, and watches as I knead it. I really lean into it, pressing into the cool squishiness, resisting the urge to punch it altogether.

"I didn't think I would, either," I admit. "But I keep my word. I have some integrity."

"So, what? You're saying I have none?"

"Well, based on your actions, I think the amount is questionable," I say, beginning to flatten the dough.

"My actions are no different than yours. You wanted to go to art club even though you weren't allowed, so you used deliveries as a way to get there. I wanted to go to study group with my friends, so I used a delivery—"

"You used *me*," I correct him. "And stop lying. That wasn't a study group."

"You're such a hypocrite," he says.

I accidentally break a hole in the crust out of frustration. Throwing the dough down and wrestling it back together, I say, "You can't be serious."

"You wanted a break from the shop to do something you like. My dad is trying to teach me interior design—which I have absolutely no interest in—and I just wanted a break—"

"You get a break, though, Justin!" I cry. Who am I kidding? I didn't come here for a pizza lesson. I came here to give Justin a piece of my mind.

"You get to do what you want most of the time. You and your dad leave the shop at least an hour before

I do. By the time I get home, I'm supposed to find time to have dinner, do homework, and still have enough energy to do my art."

"It's not my fault your parents don't give you a lot of freedom."

"But it *is* your fault that you keep acting like our situations are the same," I snap, throwing the repaired corn bread crust into the pan.

"How are they different, then? *Enlighten* me, Maya." His tone is sarcastic, but I don't care.

"I feel like nothing is mine right now," I blurt. "Hempstead isn't my home. My room doesn't feel like my room. I have control over nothing, and I hate it. Art is the one thing that gives me peace. It's the one thing that I was able to control. And yes, I use deliveries as a cover for me getting less than twenty minutes to myself—but it's *my* twenty minutes. And you tried to take that from me. Actually, you might not have taken away art club, but you did take away that little bit of control that I had. You left me with nothing, even though I confided in you."

Justin frowns, holding my gaze. "Have you tried

talking to your parents and telling them how important art club is to you?"

"What do you think?" I ask. "They said no. All they care about is the precious grand opening. So, no, I haven't tried talking to them *again*." I shake my head in disbelief. *Of course* he would ask that question. "I don't expect you to understand."

"What's that supposed to mean?" he asks.

I shove the pan into the oven and then grab a mixing bowl out of the cabinet. Retrieving a whisk from a pitcher on the counter behind me, I say, "Because you get everything you want. You live in a huge house, your parents don't ask you to work, you have one of the prettiest girls at school falling all over you and a million friends because you've lived here your whole life. You have everything and have no reason to care about anyone but yourself because caring about you seems to get you anything and everything—"

"No, I don't," he says.

I pour a can of candied yams into the bowl with brown sugar and a little bit of cream. "Yes . . . you . . . do," I say, whisking so hard my entire body shakes.

"You don't know anything about me, Maya."

"Tell . . . me . . . then."

I keep my attention focused on whipping the cream because I'm in no mood to ask him where he keeps the pots so I can simmer it.

Justin starts speaking quickly, his eyes on the floor. "I want to be a chef, and I feel like I can't do that without disappointing my parents. My dad built his design firm from the ground up and says I'm supposed to take it over someday. Like, he planned my life before I was old enough to walk. He has this whole idea for my life and failing to fit into that makes me feel like a failure."

"Your dad can't force you to be an interior designer," I say, since he's acting like he doesn't know this. "Okay, so you tag along for some consultations and learn something. When you're old enough, you get to do what you want to do."

"Maya, come on—"

"No. See? That's what I mean, you keep making it seem like our problems are the same, but yours is superficial. You don't want to learn from your dad because you want to cook. And since you're such a good cook, why am I here giving you pizza lessons?"

"You know what? I don't know!" he shouts.

The volume of his voice catches me off guard, and I step back.

"You're so fake," I say quietly, swallowing hard to keep my tears from falling.

Looking up, Justin's face has gone from defensive to hurt. I can't take it. I can't believe there was a part of me that thought he was cute and smart and more than what I originally assumed. I was kidding myself, thinking that we could be friends.

I don't even grab any of my supplies, I just leave. Outside, tears start falling and I have to remind myself not to miss the step on the walkway.

A wave of déjà vu hits me as I approach my bike, feeling the same way I did two weeks ago.

"Maya, wait!" Justin calls. His voice is pleading—for what, I have no idea.

I sit down, using the hem of my shirt to dry my face before using my heel to lift the kickstand.

"My parents are divorced," Justin says, standing at the end of his walkway, breathing heavy. "My parents got divorced over the summer, and no one knows."

More tears fall, but I don't move to wipe them. I don't move at all except to press my kickstand back to the ground. I keep my eyes on the street in front of me, telling myself I can pull off whenever I want to, that I don't have to stay.

When I don't say anything, he goes on. "My mom travels so much that my parents decided instead of her moving out and buying a new house, she can just stay with us when she's in town. And I hate it, I hate that she can just pass through whenever she wants and my dad and I are stuck here in this house living in the memory of how everything used to be while she is free to live a new life . . . without us.

"And it's not an excuse for anything. But that day that you came with the pizza, she had left again and I was mad. I took it out on you, and that was wrong. Sometimes I get so frustrated, and that day I just lost it. After you left, I took something of hers and broke it. I didn't know that my dad had given it to her, and when he got home and saw, he was totally shattered.

"He says that 'we'll be okay' and 'we'll get through

this together,' but I don't know. Honestly, Maya, the biggest reason he's making me come to the pizza shop is because he doesn't trust me to be at home by myself after school anymore. He's scared, and it makes me scared. And I don't want any of my friends to know."

I take a deep breath, still unsure what to say. Unsure if there's anything I even *want* to say.

"Dad and I had been spending so much time together, and it was suffocating me," Justin goes on. "And after last weekend, I just needed a break. And it's not an excuse, I know. And I'm sorry, Maya. But I just—I wanted some time to hang out. I needed my own twenty minutes, and I thought you would understand."

I feel like a new weight has been rested on my shoulders.

"How was I supposed to understand without you telling me any of this?" I ask.

Justin deflates, admitting, "I don't know."

"Have you talked to your dad about it?" I ask, since that's the first thing he asked me about my problems.

"I don't even know what I'm supposed to say to

him," he admits. "I tried telling him that I was fine and I wasn't going to break anything else."

We fall silent.

"I know it has nothing to do with me, but no one asked me how I felt about them splitting up," Justin adds. "Like, how it might make me feel to have my family fall apart and then pretend to be taped back together. So, I get it, the control thing. They shipped me away for half the summer so I wouldn't be here to see it, the divorce. I got home and almost all of my mom's stuff was gone, and it was like I wasn't allowed to react."

I know that feeling. Only, I had a whole summer to process everything, to get my bearings and say my goodbyes. I can't imagine what it might've been like if I got home one day and magically my entire life in Brooklyn was boxed up without explanation—without closure.

I'm torn between sympathizing with Justin and feeling like knowing all of this makes his actions worse. He understands what I've been going through and still did what he did. To have your whole life turned upside down, and then to hear that someone you barely know is going through the same thing and hardly seems to care.

"You're right, that it's not an excuse," I say after a moment.

"I'm sorry."

"Me too," I say before pushing off from the curb and pedaling away.

chapter 13

"Why does it seem like my disasters simply serve to amuse you these days?" I ask.

For the past fifteen minutes, Sasha and I have been discussing the whole Justin drama while I scroll through Etsy looking for dollhouse furniture.

Sasha, meanwhile, has slept in until noon, so she's just getting ready for her day.

"Your life is like a TV show," she says, though it comes out garbled since she's brushing her teeth. "*The Hempstead Happenings.*"

"OMG." I laugh. It's funny because it's ridiculous. "It would be more like *Hempstead Horrors.*"

"Oh, come on, it's not that bad," she says after she spits and rinses. "You went to a real pool party, with cute flirty guys and one of the most popular girls at your school. Sounds like life is *so hard* right now."

"It *is*," I say, half sarcastic and half serious. I guess she does have a point. We used to dream about going to the kinds of parties we'd see in movies and always figured they wouldn't be as dramatic until we got to high school.

"I think you guys will work this out," she reasons, going back into her bedroom.

"What is there to work out?" I ask, noticing that the only dollhouse pizza ovens are brick and not industrial. Just another thing I'll have to make myself.

"You and Justin's relationship," Sasha says, like it's obvious.

"What *relationship*?"

"The one where you clearly like him and he does the most to spend time with you—"

"Did you not hear the story I just told in which he did *the most* to spend time with Waverly?" I ask, a little incredulous that she's still on this. "And *I* do not like *him*."

"Come on, Maya. He's all you talk about."

"Not true."

"True," she says flatly. "All I ever heard about Devin is that she has green hair and likes cabbage—promising qualities, but still . . ."

"Okay, fine, so maybe—as the biggest problem in my life—I do spend a lot of time trying to figure out how to get rid of him."

"If the biggest problem in your life right now is a boy liking you, that's a pretty good life."

"Oh, come on. He *used* me!"

"Okay, but for a reason. Look at the big picture. I wouldn't be surprised if he never shares another feeling with anyone ever again."

"That's dramatic," I say, though I realize I'm not entirely convinced. "Do you really think it was that bad?"

"Sis, this boy told you that his parents split up and he feels scared and you rode off into the sunset on your bike."

"It was afternoon, with the sun high in the sky," I remind her, though she does have a point.

I can't imagine what it would be like if my parents

split. Even though the move has been hard, at least we all came together—no one left behind.

"Don't get me wrong," she continues, "things aren't easy for you right now, and I feel for you and miss you— don't you ever forget that. But after the opening, you can do art club and hopefully make more friends."

As Sasha says this, I sit down in my desk chair, slightly floored. Even though I can't change the fact that we moved, I can still pick up the pieces and start over. Justin can't start over his parents' relationship. He can't make his mom come home.

"I guess I did leave him hangin'," I admit.

"I think you owe him a text at the very least," Sasha says.

"I still don't think he likes me," I say, watching Sasha begin to take out her braids.

"Right, of course not. That's why you're the only one who knows his biggest secret."

"I miss you, too," I say, jumping back to what she said earlier.

Sasha sticks her tongue out at me, which makes me laugh.

With her hair out, Sasha gets up and repositions her phone so that I have a view of her closet—which she promptly starts to sift through in search of something other than her pink penguin pajamas to wear.

"Seriously, though," she says, her back to me. "At the end of the day, he's just trying to get you to talk to your parents."

"They already said no," I remind her.

"Yeah, like two seconds after you guys moved and they had just opened the shop. Since then, they've hired a couple more workers and you said they liked the driver they interviewed. Things are picking up and getting less chaotic, so maybe it would be worth asking again."

"I don't like this," I say, moaning. Sasha turns around, and I roll my eyes at her to let her know I'm playing. "You and Justin should not agree on this many things."

She smiles, shaking her head at me.

Taking *their* advice into account, I figure I have nothing to lose from talking to my parents again. I mean, the worst-case scenario is already my reality.

The next day during my Soul Slice shift, I come back in after making a delivery and find my parents together in the office.

"Do you have a minute?" I ask, though I'm already closing the door behind me.

"Sure, kid, what's up?" Dad grabs the other office chair and pulls it up next to Mom's so he can sit down.

"I was thinking that, since you guys hired a few more crew members and that driver, maybe we can start cutting my hours? At least, maybe we can on Wednesdays so I can go to art club after school."

"Honey," Mom says, leaning on the *y* at the end. "We already talked about waiting until after the opening."

I start to deflate, feeling more disappointed than before.

"Well, hold on. She does have a point," Dad says. "I mean, the drivers are going to have to take over her routes within the next couple weeks anyways, so it wouldn't hurt to have them do it now."

"Maybe," Mom says slowly.

"How about we look at the schedule and think about it," Dad suggests.

It's not a yes, but it's not a no, either.

"Thanks," I say, feeling my mood pick up.

I clock out and ride my bike home, noticing a slight chill in the air and the pink creeping over the horizon. There are kids running around with a dog on a front lawn at one house, and I notice an older couple sitting in rocking chairs on a porch. Farther into my neighborhood, there are lanterns at the end of every walkway, and at dusk, they begin to light up, creating a runway down the street.

My neighborhood. That's something I'm going to have to get used to. Even though Brooklyn will always be where I came from, Hempstead is slowly turning into my home.

When I get to the house, I roll my bike into the backyard and close the gate. I pull out my phone to text Mom that I made it home, but see that she already texted me.

Let me know what you think about the present on your bed.

I run upstairs to my room and push through the door, finding a beautiful batik-print fabric neatly folded on top of my comforter. There's a Post-it stuck to it that says *I thought I'd try making a dress that's as vibrant as you.*

Looking down at the pattern of orange daisy outlines, bright against the deep purple shade of the fabric, I see the color scheme for Soul Slice 2.0 collected into one perfect batik.

My heart full, I text Mom back, *I love it.*

chapter 14

With just over a week left before the festival, Devin and I have been using all our free time to work in Mr. Chris's room. I couldn't find any miniature industrial pizza ovens online, and all the dollhouse dining tables and chairs looked like something from an antique mall. So, Mr. Chris and I figure out how I can make *everything* for the model.

He gives me balsa wood scraps to make the tables and chairs, and I use acrylics to paint more poster board to make the countertops. I think I'm most excited to make the oven out of clay, paint it with glaze, and fire it in the kiln to have a nice shimmer.

While Devin and I work side by side in the art room, we ask each other questions and talk. It keeps us from getting sucked so deep into our art that we forget to eat lunch. So far, we've covered weirdest dream, best vacation, and a bug we couldn't be locked in a room with and one we could.

"What's your favorite band?" Devin asks today, hunched over a sheet of fabric that she's been gluing her magazine cutouts to.

Last week at art club, she put together a wire frame that is a life-size three-dimensional outline of her. Mr. Chris even told us that he got spooked one morning when he came into the classroom because he thought someone was standing in the corner. Now she's assembling the collages on fabric that she'll lay over the frame. Seeing Devin's project coming together makes me more excited as I get further on mine.

"That depends on the mood I'm in," I answer, gluing a clear piece of plastic wrap to the back of my convection oven door to make the window. "But I like Noname and Ari Lennox. I feel like you can't go wrong with them."

"Never heard of them," Devin admits. "How about

we make a deal? I'll listen to some of their music if you listen to some K-pop?"

Teasing, I say, "Oh, I don't know if I'm really up for making deals—seeing how that's been going for me lately."

"Ha ha ha," she says, her voice monotone. Then she gets a sly smile and adds, "Maya *Angelou*."

"I told you that in confidence," I gasp, lightly bopping her on the head with a mini countertop.

"Oh, look, I'm not the only one who wants to kill you," Waverly's voice slithers in from the doorway. She slips into the art room followed by a girl I recognize from art club (well, from the brief moments I've stolen during art club while making my pizza deliveries).

"Oh, look, it's my less impressive model," Devin says, her voice rising a few octaves to feign a pleasant tone.

Waverly just gives her the stank eye as she follows her friend to the other side of the room.

Even though we don't ask, Waverly shares with us that "Chloe's dad is one of the biggest donors for the arts program. He's the reason that losers like you—"

"Waverly," Mr. Chris says, startling all of us.

Usually he doesn't pay attention to what's going on because he has his headphones on and his nose in the school paper. Then again, maybe the headphones are a front and he's always listening . . .

"Do I hear bullying in my classroom?" he asks, raising his eyebrows.

Waverly flashes a sweet smile. "Excuse me, Mr. Chris. What I meant to say was that Chloe's dad is the reason *artists* like you get to . . . do what you *do*."

Her eyes dart from us back to Mr. Chris. He gives Waverly a look but then nods and puts his headphones back over his ears.

"You say that like it's a bad thing," I note, watching as Chloe sifts through the project cubbies and surfaces with a sculpture of her own. It's a clay blowfish teapot with thick lips and spikes all over.

"*When* Chloe wins," Waverly goes on, "her dad is going to take us to a new Greek restaurant that opened in Center City. Much better than pizza, don't you think?" Waverly asks, smiling her fake smile.

Her eyes lock on mine, and I flash back to her

dissing my parents' pizza at the pool party. I also flash back to how close Justin was sitting next to her at the edge of the pool, and something inside me drops a little.

"You don't know that Chloe is going to win," Devin says before I can come up with a snarky response. When Chloe looks up from counting the spikes on her blowfish, Devin adds, "No offense."

I'm distracted by her set of matching blowfish teacups with fins for handles.

"Well, she won last year," Waverly points out.

"That doesn't guarantee she's going to win this year. You guys don't even know what projects are being entered," Devin argues.

Devin and Waverly's identical glares mirror each other from across the room.

"Well, at the very least, I know her project is better than your sorry excuse for a lawn ornament," Waverly snaps, "and *her* cardboard pizza hut."

As much as I want to tell her to not call it a pizza hut, I know that it'll only make her say it more. Instead, I decide to get some air and tell Devin I'm going to the bathroom.

Alone in the hallway, I realize that the image of Chloe, her dad, and Waverly going out to dinner after the festival reminded me that my parents might not even come. I mean, they don't exactly know about it yet—

"Maya?"

I whip around and see Justin standing outside the doorway to the stairwell.

"You okay?" he asks.

I never called or texted after we talked on Saturday, after he revealed his secret.

"Are *you* okay?" I ask, though he probably has no idea that I'm loading my words with meaning: how he's been since his mom left and what he's been doing to cope, why he's kept it to himself.

Wondering *and* worrying.

But I don't say any of it.

"I'm cool . . ." he admits, though the last word hangs in the air, his sentence feeling incomplete.

In the empty space between us, in the growing silence, I find the opening to say something—*anything*—about everything he shared with me.

"Waverly is in Mr. Chris's room with Chloe" are the only words that come out of my mouth.

"Thanks," he says, and with that, he turns on his heel and disappears into the art room.

Somehow, I feel further away from Justin than ever, and that makes me realize he's someone that I wanted to be close to.

❤

That night, I make a point of wandering down the hall to my parents' room once we're all showered and relaxed after dinner. I find them in their usual places on their bed, Dad reading a book and Mom flipping through a magazine during the commercials of whatever ABC sitcom she's watching on TV.

Their room is set up different from how it was in Brooklyn. It flows better, with the dressers pushed together to make a base for their TV, and they have nightstands now so that their love seat isn't cluttered with mail and papers. There are still boxes lining the room, a physical reminder of how much work they've done settling in at the shop instead of settling in at home.

"Hey, sweetie," Dad says when he looks up from his book and finds me in the doorway.

I cross the room and sink down into the love seat at the end of their bed.

"Guess what," I say, waiting until I have Mom's attention, too.

I get through the whole explanation of what the art festival is and how I've been putting together my project without revealing any details of my art club attendance.

"The festival is next week, and it would be really cool if you guys could be there. That way you could see my project. And maybe I'll win an award or something."

"Next week?" Dad says, scrunching his brows together. He and Mom exchange a look that doesn't make me feel like I can get my hopes up.

"What day is it?" Mom asks, both of them staring me down expectantly.

"The twenty-fourth."

By the way they deflate I can tell this is somehow the wrong answer.

"Honey, we were going to tell you tomorrow after we talk to Justin's dad, but we're opening next week."

"What?" I can't help but laugh a little. "You guys haven't even picked out tables and chairs."

"Actually, we have," Mom says, smiling. It's the biggest smile I've seen from her in ages. She's been so tired, her patience stretched thin from all she's been handling at the shop—finding people to hire, making sure supply orders get processed on time now that we're contracted with new companies from the area. From this smile alone, I figure this must be good.

"Well, spill."

"Do you remember the suggestions you made that first day Justin's dad was at the shop?"

"Yes ..."

"We decided to go with the retro look. Justin actually suggested some chairs to us and found tables to match online."

"Justin? When?" I ask, going around to Mom's side of the bed when she pulls out her phone.

"Today, when he was in the office with us at the shop," Dad says.

When Mom turns her phone around, my suspicions are confirmed. Justin totally found furniture that matches my sketches that he saw. Then he went behind my back and suggested it to my parents . . . but he did it without giving away my whole art project.

"Justin *suggested* these?" I ask, still stuck on that.

"Yeah. When he showed it to us, it just felt right. And I think we were sold because he reminded us that this is what you thought of in the first place," Dad says, clearly proud and satisfied with this decision.

"Maya, honey." Mom reels me in since I'm still a little scattered. I focus on her. "We are *so* proud of you and happy that you've gotten involved and are going to be in the art show. But we're set to open on the twenty-fourth and we need you at Soul Slice so we can welcome Hempstead as a family."

I can't believe this. Holding on to my last bit of hope, I take what Justin and Sasha have been saying into my heart.

"The festival is really important to me," I say. "Art has been the one thing that's truly mine since we moved. I really want to be there, and I really want you guys to be there. We don't even have to stay for the whole event."

"Is the festival just that one day?" Dad asks.

"Well, no. But that's opening night—when the judging happens," I tell them, fiddling with a loose thread hanging from the hem of my pajama shirt.

"Do you have to be standing next to your piece for the judging?" Mom asks.

I know what they're doing. They're setting me up so that they can rationalize me missing the festival and make it seem like the perfect compromise for them to come see the show on another night. And I hate it, because technically they're right. But I won't get another opening day. I want to be there.

"Look, we know that this has been hard on you," Dad says, setting his book on his nightstand. "That's not lost on us, and we really appreciate everything that you've sacrificed for the shop. We promise that after we get through the opening, everything will go back to normal."

I sigh because I have nothing to say. No comeback,

no argument to try to help my case. This is it. Once again, it's been decided that what matters to me comes second to the shop. *Their* shop, to be specific. Soul Slice isn't mine to make sacrifices for, and yet, I feel like I'm the one who's had to give up the most.

chapter 15

"I can't believe I'm not going to the art festival," I say the next afternoon, leaning back against one of the pillars on Devin's porch. It might not be my favorite Brooklyn brownstone stoop with the slight dip in the concrete that makes it feel specifically shaped for someone to sit on, but Devin's front steps work just fine as a venting place.

Seeing how they've disappointed me once again, my dad figured a fair trade-off would be to let me go home from work early today. Instead, I decided to use my freedom to go see Devin so that I wouldn't have to sit in my room in a puddle of my hopelessness alone.

"The Soul Slice grand opening better be worth it," Devin says, slumping against her own pillar. Then she straightens up, pointing to something in the distance. "Maya, look."

I glance down the street, and I see Justin jogging toward us. *What?* He stops in front of the steps, doubles over with his hands on his knees, and starts huffing and puffing.

"Have you ever thought about running track instead of playing baseball in the spring?" I ask, Devin and I trying to stifle our laughter.

"I Ha," he says, pausing to take a breath. "Ha." Takes another breath. "Ha."

"What are you doing here anyway?" I ask.

"I asked . . . my dad . . . if I . . . could come . . . after . . . you," he huffs, struggling to stand up straight.

"You didn't have to run," I say, though part of me— deep on the inside and unrevealed—is flattered that he did.

"Well, you seemed pretty upset when you left Soul Slice," he reasons, leaning against my pillar.

Afraid that sweat might fall on me, I discreetly scoot over a little.

"Yeah, well, I'm not allowed to go to the art festival

because I have to work at the opening," I explain.

"Wait, you're kidding, right?" he asks, brows scrunched together.

I look up at him, squinting into the sun. "No," I say.

"I thought you were upset about your parents not coming," he explains. "Getting you to the festival is the easy part."

"It is?" Devin and I exchange a glance, confused.

"Don't tell me you've chosen *now* to lose your edge," Justin says, laughing. "Maya, just have Devin order a pizza to the school."

Wait. He's right. *How* did we not think of that?

I open my mouth to say something, but then Devin looks at Justin and says, "You know, if you weren't all sweaty and gross, I could kiss you right now—well, that and the fact that Waverly would probably stab me with her comb in my sleep."

As morbid as that sounds, the mental image is hilarious.

"It'll be the last sneak-around before the opening, and hopefully I'll never have to do it again," I say, feeling confident and buzzing from the fact that Justin was already thinking two steps ahead . . . about me.

We plot the specifics. Devin will order a pizza under her name but use the address of the house next to the school so that my parents won't get suspicious; Justin will get permission from his dad to leave the Soul Slice grand opening early so that he can head over to the school before me; I'll take the delivery, meet up with Justin outside the girls' bathroom, where he will hand me a prepacked bag with my dress and shoes so that I can change and go to the showroom in time for the judging; then I'll leave, change back into my uniform, and hustle back to Soul Slice for the rest of opening night.

With all of us on the same page, and me no longer wallowing in self-pity, I figure I should take advantage of my afternoon off and go home to get some homework done. Justin offers to walk with me and we say goodbye to Devin, finding ourselves suddenly in charged silence.

At least, it's charged for me.

"I'm sorry," I say, figuring I should start there.

"For what?"

"For not saying anything after you told me about your mom," I say.

Justin nods. "You don't have to apologize."

"I do, though, because I vented to you and you at least tried to be there for me. You told me your biggest secret, and I just left you standing there. I feel bad."

Thinking about this for a moment, Justin finally says, *"I don't need your pity,"* in a high-pitched voice meant to imitate me.

"Hey!" I shout, letting go of my handlebars to shove him.

Without keeping the wheel straight, my bike swerves into me. But Justin catches it before the front wheel can scrape my shin.

"Seriously, though," he says once we both stop laughing. He takes my bike and starts pushing it, looking down at the wheel rolling over the cracks in the sidewalk. "I wanted to tell someone, but I just couldn't. Maybe that's shallow, not wanting my friends to know what's really going on. I've always been Justin who lives in the big house; whose mom is kind of famous— if you know anything about architecture, I guess; who has a dad that shows up to all his games, and a picture-perfect life. It wasn't until that all fell apart that I realized how much it mattered to me—"

"That doesn't make you shallow," I say. "'Picture perfect' *was* your life, and—like you said—it suddenly went away. You had every right—you *have* every right—to be upset."

"I guess I thought if I didn't tell anyone, then I could pretend like nothing had changed—at least, not outside my house."

"I get that," I say.

"Yeah, but then you came along," he says, smiling to himself. To me, he adds, "Riding in on your *hot wheels*."

"What*ever*," I say, pretending to be annoyed and rolling my eyes.

"You pulled up with the grossest pizza—pepperoni *and* black olives," he says ruefully. But then serious again, he continues, "And I was rude to you. I took my frustration out on you, and it was like a piece of the truth slipped out that day. That wasn't me. I felt bad, and I wanted to apologize, but then *you* were stubborn and refused . . . and then I found out why. Your life had been turned upside down, too. You understood."

I nod, glancing at him. "I do understand."

"And I realized after last Saturday that someone else would understand, too," Justin says, looking back at me. "My dad got left, too, you know. Like, I hadn't even thought of that. Even though he and Mom decided to get a divorce together, he stayed with me and she's out there. Both of us are stuck where we are, together."

I think about my parents. I wasn't the only one who uprooted my life. My parents took a risk, too, and left behind the place that's been their home longer than I've been alive. They didn't have friends in Hempstead, either. I've been mostly blaming them in my head for their decision instead of doing my best to support them—inside and outside of Soul Slice.

"Did you talk to your dad?" I ask, hopeful.

"Yeah. Talking doesn't fix everything, but it's a start. Telling him that we don't have to pretend to hold everything together helped us somehow, like we see each other."

"I'm happy for you," I say, meaning it.

"I wish that your parents could be more

understanding," he says as we come to a stop at the end of my driveway.

"I think they are as understanding as they need to be," I admit. "They're right, that in a little more than a week we'll finally jump over the biggest hurdle and I'll go back to being their daughter instead of their employee. My stuff isn't permanent; I've just been impatient—I guess."

It feels weird, trying to see things from my parents' side, but it helps. It makes them seem less like they're set against me and my happiness and more like they're truly trying their best—which is all I can really ask.

"I feel like you're a good daughter. You're definitely a hardworking employee. And you're a really good friend, Maya," Justin says, leaning my bike toward me.

I take the handlebars, the weight of the bike feeling different as it stands as an object between us.

"You're a good friend, too," I say, feeling bittersweet.

"Thanks," Justin says. He smiles, waves, and walks off toward his house.

I watch him go. It's taken us so long to get to this point, but a greedy part of me feels like I want more.

chapter 16

My parents close Soul Slice for the weekend to let the painters finish up. When I step into the shop on Monday after school, I'm stunned by the transformation. Soul Slice 2.0 is completely its own, designed and decorated from the ground up.

We have purple walls with orange trim, a counter decorated in orange daisies, and a ceiling finished with dangling balls of fairy lights. A purple soda fountain has been installed, alongside a few arcade games. Framed photographs from the old shop, sent as a gift from the employees back in Brooklyn, hang on the walls. There's a picture of my parents when they were younger and first opened Reynolds' Pizza, another one of them holding me as a baby and comparing me to the size of a puffy sweet Corn Bread Crust pizza, and then a final one of us when I was in elementary school, standing under the first Soul Slice sign after the name changed.

The shop is soulful, original, and perfect. The best part is feeling all three of us represented: my dad's carefreeness, my mom's organization, and my love of vibrant standout colors.

The furniture arrives, and Justin, our parents, Devin, and I work together to set up the tables and chairs for ideal customer flow.

Pushing in the final two chairs, Justin admits, "This isn't too far from your version, you know."

Looking at the orange tables and matching retro diner chairs, I can't say he's wrong.

"You say it like it's a coincidence," I say, buzzing.

My mini Soul Slice model has come together as well. During lunchtime today, I painted my clay pizza oven with glaze, using a tiny brush to get all the little details like knobs and handles. Mr. Chris is going to fire it in the kiln, and I can't wait to see it.

Devin, Justin, and I slip into the seats at our last

table, exhausted from unpacking and moving so many things bigger than ourselves. I watch as Mom trains the cashiers behind the fully functioning counter. The now *four* delivery drivers file in and out of the shop like clockwork.

"Thank you, guys, for helping," I say with my eyes closed.

"You know what would be a *real* thank-you?" Devin asks, prompting me to open one of my eyes.

"What?"

"Some pizza," she says, looking over her shoulder toward the kitchen, where the culmination of sweet, smoky, and savory aromas are in heavy rotation.

I take a deep breath and find the energy to haul myself out of my chair. Even if Devin didn't ask, I've actually had a surprise up my sleeve this whole time.

I get permission from my parents to let Devin and Justin come in the back, and Dad files in behind us. They each get situated in an apron and plastic gloves before Dad returns with a metal container.

"What's this?" Devin asks, rubbing her hands together.

"This is braised short rib," I say, locking eyes with Justin. "Slow-cooked on our grill at home."

Justin's eyes light up with recognition.

"Now, you guys are going to make the pizza and teach me," Dad explains. Then to Justin, he adds, "If it's okay with you, we want to include this pizza in our menu for the grand opening."

"Really?" Justin asks, his whole face breaking into a huge smile.

"Yes! Maya told us you had this idea, and it's brilliant. It's a great new twist, and it carries the heart of Soul Slice," Dad says, clapping Justin on the shoulder. "We'd give you credit, of course."

"Thank you so much, Mr. Reynolds. This is awesome. Oh my gosh, my idea is going to be on the menu," Justin gushes, looking around at all of us like he doesn't know what to do with himself. I grin, feeling proud of him.

We work together, turning Justin's idea into a masterpiece pizza. We pick toppings, Justin taking the lead based on what he thinks will pair well with the ribs, and then I season the crust before sliding it into the oven. With Justin and Devin flicking their wrists and sprinkling toppings unevenly but in their own way, I realize I've never had this much fun making a pizza. The only thing that could make this day better is if Sasha were here, too.

When the pizza is ready, Justin, Devin, and I carry it to a table and sit down to feast. I take a bite of my slice, and it's delicious—the perfect amount of smoky and savory. Justin really might be a great chef someday, and when I tell him that, his whole face lights up.

"Well," Dad says as he and Mom come over to our table with a tray of vanilla Cokes. "To our first dine-in Hempstead Soul Slice customers, we'd like to say thank you."

"Not only for helping out today, but for putting a smile on Maya's face," Mom adds.

"*Mom,*" I moan, covering my face with my hands.

"I don't know who she'd be without us," Justin teases.

"A lost soul, for sure," Devin joins in, laughing.

Peeking out between my fingers, I realize I couldn't have asked for better friends than Justin and Devin to help show me the way.

"So, maybe *The Hempstead Happenings* is more like a movie than a TV show," Sasha says when we're FaceTiming a couple nights later on festival eve. "Because all the drama is over and there's not enough material to make a whole show."

"Thank *God*." I break down laughing. "I don't think I could take any more."

"I'm happy for you," she says. "Part of me thought I would be salty about you leaving and, like, having this whole new life without me. But I'm not."

"Really?" I ask, grabbing my phone from where I have it leaned against a couple books on my desk and bringing it closer.

"Yeah. I've been in Brooklyn my whole life. I would kill to go somewhere new, and here you are getting a fresh start. I don't know, maybe I was jealous—"

"I was jealous of *you*," I say, feeling relieved. "I leave, and two seconds later, you get a date to the Snowflake dance *and* a boyfriend."

Mentioning Jeffrey makes her blush, and I realize I'm happy to see her happy.

"It was *one* date," she says, still blushing.

"The first of many," I remind her. "I'm happy for you, too."

She pouts her bottom lip the same way she did on my last day in Brooklyn. It's not a sad pout so much as a sentimental one.

"I really hope you win the art contest."

"I'll try my best," I say, unable to stop smiling. "Tomorrow, I put the last piece into the mini Soul Slice."

"Yeah?"

"It went in the kiln this afternoon," I say.

After figuring out how to make all the furniture and appliances myself, I realized that one of the best things about my project is how it incorporates different art mediums. There's sculpture, design, painting, and even a little woodworking.

"I bet it will be amazing, like all the other art you do," she says matter-of-factly.

"Thanks, Sasha."

A knock at my door pulls my attention away.

Mom is standing there, holding up the finished dress.

"Gotta go," I say to Sasha.

"In a while, alligator," she says, winking.

"See you later, crocodile."

"How is Sasha?" Mom asks, coming into my room and sitting at the foot of my bed.

I swivel around in my desk chair to face her. "She's good. She has a date to the Snowflake dance this year, so that's exciting."

"Oh, let her know that if she wants, I can make her a dress."

"I will," I say, though my focus is on the dress in her hand.

Mom holds up the dress for me to see. It has spaghetti straps and a straight-across neckline. The torso cinches in at the waist, and there's a circle skirt that I can already tell will be fun to twirl in.

"Wow," I say, standing up to take the dress from her. "It's gorgeous. Thank you, Mom."

"Maya," she says, her tone serious and her voice quiet. I look her in the eye. "Your father and I, we love you so much."

"Mom, I know *that*," I say. "I love you, too."

"And you're so talented and bright. We just know that you're going to grow up and do amazing things because you're so passionate."

"Do you guys want me to take over the shop one day?" I ask, thinking of Justin and his dad.

A laugh kind of busts out of her, like she wasn't even trying to laugh but couldn't help it.

"Maya," she says, "honey, we don't want you to because *you* don't want to."

I scoff, pretending to be offended. "How do you know that?"

"Because pizza isn't your passion. You're good at it, and cooking is in your blood. But it's not what you're meant to do—and that's okay. No matter how successful your father and I are, we will always want more for you. We want you to follow your dreams, Maya."

I close the space between us and give her a hug. Even though I do feel a little guilty about sneaking around, and that I'll be dipping out of the opening tomorrow, I think in some way that's the "more" my mom is talking about. She just doesn't realize it.

chapter 17

"No way!" I shout, running up to Devin. It's the morning of the art festival, and she's standing outside Mr. Chris's room, waiting with some other kids for him to unlock the door. "I love your hair!"

Devin's dyed her hair dark purple, and it looks great, especially paired with her bright orange hoop earrings.

"Thanks," she says with a grin. "And this is Maya," she tells the other kids. "Her parents own Soul Slice, so be there at—what time is the opening?"

"Five," I say.

As Mr. Chris unlocks the door and we all file inside, I tell Devin, "Thank you for being amazing."

"No, Fried Chicken and Waffle pizza is *amazing*,"

she corrects me before retrieving her self-portrait from the far corner of the room.

I pull my model down from its place on top of the project cubbies. I set it on the table next to Devin. I still can't believe that I managed to put this together in just a few weeks. Justin is right; the model does look a lot like the real Soul Slice, and somehow that makes it even better.

Mr. Chris comes over to us with a small box containing my final pieces. In addition to sculpting the oven out of clay, I even made little people to position around the shop. I modeled them after the real Soul Slice employees. The little Denise one even has a nail file and Bantu knots.

"Good news and bad news," Mr. Chris says, not setting the box down.

"What?" I ask, knowing it has to be serious since Mr. Chris's glasses are in front of his eyes instead of on his forehead.

"So, your crew turned out well with their limbs and their heads and stuff, but the oven . . ."

"What happened with the oven?" I ask, beginning to panic.

Mr. Chris finally sets the box down, and I look inside. The oven is in pieces.

"Sometimes pieces break in the kiln. We could try to glue it back together," he says, though I can hear the doubt in his voice.

"Then it'll *look* broken," I say, pulling the parts out of the box and laying them on the table, a lump in my throat.

The oven is shattered. It would take forever to try to piece it back together, and even then, I don't think there's a way to put the tiny chipped pieces back on without the glue seeping through. Despair creeps into the corners of my mind, but I fight to hold it off. I've come too far to quit now over one piece. I take the figurines off the box and put the pieces of the oven back inside. Admiring what's intact, I know in my gut that this doesn't have to be the end of the world. Everything else turned out perfect.

"I'm going to have to figure something out," I tell Mr. Chris, though I know my options are limited. If I don't have enough time to glue the oven back together, then I definitely don't have enough time to make a new one. To Devin, who is making my Denise statue kiss the Jean one, I whisper, "I have no idea what to do."

"Don't worry about it," she says in a high-pitched voice, holding mini Denise in front of my head. "Devin can figure something out while you're at work." Then she holds up the Jean statue and says in a deep voice, "Yeah, that Devin is so cool and resourceful. I'm so glad you made a friend, *and on your first day*."

"Jean, don't make me fire you," I tease. "But seriously, do you think there's something you can figure out in time?"

"Yes. All I ask is that you put extra fried chicken on my scheme pizza."

"Done," I say, thankful and glad that I know I can put full faith in Devin because she always comes through.

After almost a month of walking to the shop either with Devin or Justin, it feels weird to ride my bike there alone. Justin's dad is picking him up from school to take him home so that he can change before the grand opening. Devin is at school, putting the finishing touches on her piece and doing whatever she can to fix my oven situation. So, I roll to a stop at Soul Slice in record time.

Inside the shop, the air is buzzing. There are purple streamers dangling from the ceiling, a huge glittery GRAND OPENING sign hangs above the counter, and chalkboard signs are hung up around the shop with detailed illustrations of our signature pizzas. There's even one with Justin's BBQ rib pizza.

"Heads up!"

I turn around as Denise rounds the corner from the kitchen, tossing me a purple employee T-shirt. I catch it and maneuver it around so that the collar is in my hand and the rest of the shirt unfurls.

"Whoa." My name is embroidered on the right side with an orange pepperoni pizza outline next to it. "This is so cool."

"I know, right? Check how this purple matches my nail polish."

I lean in to look at Denise's purple ombré nails.

"Those are really cool."

"Thanks," she says, smiling wide.

"Thank you, too," I say, resisting the sudden urge to hug her.

"What for?" she asks, ignoring the ping of the delivery monitor.

"Well, you were the first person—coworker, I guess—to really talk to me. The old Soul Slice felt like family, and I felt like an outsider here."

"Girl, us drivers have to stick together," Denise says, holding out a fist for me to bump.

I head to the bathroom and change into my employee shirt. I stash the T-shirt I wore to school in my backpack, along with my new purple-and-orange dress and a pair of sandals. When Justin gets here, I'll find a moment to give him my backpack before both of us slip out separately and make our way to school.

Since Mom managed to hire a full staff in time for today, my radius for deliveries has shrunk drastically. My school is still my domain, but if I were to get a delivery for Devin's or Justin's house, it would no longer be my responsibility.

So, I make myself busy organizing cups and straws

at the soda fountain, filling up napkin dispensers, and folding extra boxes for deliveries and takeout orders.

I find myself waiting for the sound of the bells over the door. Every time they jingle, I look up, expecting it to be Justin and his dad. This time, to my surprise, David from the pool party walks in with Carter.

"Hey, Maya Angelou," he says, his smile still charming.

"Hey, what's up, guys?"

I come out from behind the counter.

"Justin told us he and his dad are on their way. We came to show support," David explains.

"I hope it's okay that we invited some people," Carter adds.

I can't help but laugh a little. "Carter, that's the point. *Thank you.*"

"So, you really work here?" David asks, looking around and taking everything in.

"Today is my last day," I say, feeling so good about it. "My parents own the place, so I was just helping out through the opening."

"So, after today, you can come to another pool party

and not run off?" David asks, raising his eyebrows.

"Dude, knock it off. You know what Justin said," Carter mumbles, though it's loud enough that I catch it.

"What did Justin say?"

When their faces turn red, my sus meter starts going off. But I don't get a chance to interrogate them because more kids start showing up, kids that I recognize from school but haven't had the chance to talk to yet. David and Carter start introducing me, and I start answering questions about what pizzas I recommend and what sides are the best, which soda is my favorite, etc. When a few girls hold out their phones to take selfies, I hop in and ask that they use #SoulSlice to build some hype for the shop. I wish Devin was here; a picture with her purple hair would be so cool.

I realize how pleasantly ironic it is that pizza is what's finally bringing me and my classmates together. As I'm recommending pizza toppings to a group of guys from the basketball team, I completely miss Justin and his dad coming in. Justin catches me off guard, tapping me on the shoulder from behind.

"Oh my . . . gosh? Aren't you a little overdressed?" I say, finding it kinda cute that he has on a short-sleeve button-down shirt. It's purple with palm trees on it.

"My dad said that this is technically a business event for us and that I had to look the part."

"Well, then, you look incredibly professional," I say, using a hoity-toity accent.

"You don't look too bad yourself," Justin says, no accent, no humor, just his eyes staring straight into mine. "And, hey, your chin."

He reaches out, touching his thumb where my Band-Aid used to be. The scab is gone, and there's just a tiny scar, one that you wouldn't really notice unless you knew it was there.

His hand falls back to his side, and I open my mouth to say something. When nothing comes out, I try to cover it up by smiling, but I'm pretty sure it was obvious that I was at a loss for words, which is a first. Suddenly, I really wish I had my dress on right now instead of jeans and the Soul Slice T-shirt.

"Did you hear about Chloe?" Justin asks.

Chloe is the furthest thing from my mind right now, honestly.

"No?"

He pulls out his phone and shows me his texts with Devin. After confirming that he was on his way to Soul Slice, Devin sent a long text about Chloe being disqualified from the art contest because she copied a winning piece from the art show almost ten years ago. One of the eighth graders working on the school newspaper thought her project looked familiar and brought it up to Mr. Chris when they found an old photograph.

I'm floored. "Chloe seemed so innocent."

"Anyone who's friends with Waverly is decidedly *not* innocent," Justin says, laughing at his own joke.

"You're friends with Waverly," I remind him, slightly amused.

"Am I, though?" he asks, smiling slyly.

"Hello, everyone! Can I please have your attention?"

Justin and I, along with all the other kids, parents, and neighbors, turn our attention toward the counter—which Dad is standing on top of! Everyone quiets down, a few people taking the last empty seats and the rest having no choice but to stand.

"My wife, our daughter, Maya, and I would all like to thank you for coming to our grand opening," Dad says, Mom appearing behind him. We lock eyes, and she motions for me to come over, so I start weaving my way through the crowd.

"Soul Slice started out as a hole-in-the-wall shop in the heart of Brooklyn. It was our first child after my wife and I got married, and it was practically Maya's day care after she was born," he admits, making everyone laugh. "We knew it was a big endeavor, starting a new Soul Slice here in Hempstead. But this new shop is more than we could've imagined. We are so happy to be here and so grateful that you have welcomed us to your town."

Standing at the counter with my family, looking at everyone who came out to show support, I feel each of my dad's words in my heart. I recognize kids from school, adults that I've delivered to, even high schoolers who upped their tips when they pitied me on Friday nights. Though it's no Brooklyn, Hempstead is a community of people who love Soul Slice. And maybe I'm starting to love Hempstead a little bit, too.

"On behalf of my whole family, I just want to say thank you and we look forward to serving you vibrant original pizzas meant to feed the soul!" Dad finishes, patting me on the shoulder when he climbs down from the counter.

Applause breaks out, and anyone who doesn't already have a slice rushes to the counter. Even people with slices go up for seconds. My parents eat up the chaos, punching in orders like they themselves are machines. With their attention occupied, Justin and I take the perfect opportunity to sneak over to the delivery station.

I hold out my backpack to him, ready to get our plan in motion, but he stops me. Instead of grabbing the bag, he grabs my hand wrapped around the bag and holds on until I look at him.

"Good luck, Maya," he says.

His eyes look big, and suddenly the only thought I can hold in my head is how I want to drown in their honey-brown shade. Then it dawns on me that his eyes look so big because his face is so close to mine, his lips two soft pillows pulled slightly into a smile.

Is he going to kiss me?

The delivery screen pings, and Justin looks over my head at the screen.

"It's go time," he says. With that, he takes my bag and disappears into the crowd. I watch until the bells above the front door jingle with his departure.

I pull out a delivery bag and lie in wait for Devin's Fried Chicken and Waffle pizza—with extra fried chicken—to be boxed.

"I got this," Denise says when she comes around the corner and sees me at the ready.

"That's okay," I say, reaching up and tugging on the box. "It's in my jurisdiction."

She doesn't let go, and we lock eyes.

"Your parents want you *here*," she says, though something amused is dancing in her eyes.

"I don't mind," I assure her, tugging it again.

This time, she lets go of the box, but she positions herself between me and the exit.

"Does this have to do with your little boyfriend?" she asks, crossing her arms over her chest.

"I don't have a *boyfriend*," I say, zipping the bag closed and checking the time on my phone.

The festival started a little while ago, but judging is in twenty minutes.

"Then why are you and lil' dude looking all cozy together every day?" she asks, quirking her brow.

"We do *not*," I insist, trying not to blush. "Denise, please move."

I try to go around her, but she slides to the side. When I try to go the other way, she slides that way. I can't go out the back door because I'd pass the kitchen and the office and there's a very slim chance I'd make it without my parents seeing me.

"Drivers are supposed to have each other's backs, right?" I ask.

"Then you gotta spill what I'm having your back for."

"I'm in an art show at school and they're about to announce winners for the awards and I've worked super hard on my project and it has been my favorite thing about moving here and even though my parents said no I don't want to miss it so I'm using *this* delivery as cover to go attend the judging ceremony and then I'll be right back—I swear," I say, all in one gigantic breath.

"I gotchu, sis, go—get out of here," Denise says, shaking her head and pointing to the door.

She steps aside, and I duck past the counter, where two of the cashiers are now in charge, and weave through the crowd. I get squished and shoved, greeted, and asked about what I'm doing—but I have no time to stop. I slip outside, thankful for the slight chill in the evening air. With the crowd blocking the front window, I don't have to worry about getting caught as I strap the bag to the back of my bike and push off.

By the time I reach the school, I don't have time to chain my bike to the rack on the front lawn. I just lean it against the wall next to the school's entrance. Once inside, I break into a run, keeping the pizza level as I sprint down the hallways, turning a few times before finding Justin standing outside the girls' bathroom.

"Did I miss it?" I ask, quickly exchanging the pizza for my bag of clothes.

"They started announcing the painting and drawing winners. You're good," he says.

I run into a stall and slip out of my Soul Slice uniform and into the dress Mom made me. I nearly run out the bathroom without checking myself, but the bright colors catch my eye in the mirror and I stop. With my shoulders out and a slight T-shirt tan giving away all the days I've been out in the sun, the way the dress cinches in at my waist and fans out over my hips, I wonder why I've never asked Mom to make me a dress before. I feel beautiful. I do a quick twirl, and the skirt fans out into a full circle.

Pulling my T-shirt over my head ruined my half-up–half-down look, so I just take the hair tie out and let all my box braids fall around my shoulders. Perfect.

Leaving the bathroom, I step back into *Mission: Impossible* mode.

"Hold up." Justin stays, blocking me. "Devin said to make you eat a slice to calm your nerves."

"I'm calm, I'm totally calm. Suuuuper calm," I say, looking at the double doors standing between me and the gym. "Okay, maybe one slice," I relent, picking one that's not hogging too much of Devin's extra fried chicken.

I take a bite of the delicious, familiar warmth. Forcing myself to be still and chew brings my heart rate down from thundering to a calm and collected rhythm. Justin eats a slice, too, and I catch him looking at me in between bites, the two of us smiling at each other with our mouths full. If I had more time, I might let myself worry about whether or not this is all in my head—the compliments, the held eye contact, the fluttery feeling I get sometimes . . . but then someone with a microphone on the other side of the gym doors announces that they're moving on to the three-dimensional categories.

Justin stashes our pizza and my clothes behind a nearby trash can before we head inside. It's cool inside the gym; the air-conditioning clings to my exposed skin, raising goose bumps and making me feel ten times better.

As I make a beeline to where I set up my project next to Devin's, I realize how many parents are here.

A boy won first place for most realistic sketch on his collection of insect drawings, and his mom and dad are both giving him hugs. And I find Devin standing next to her collage self-portrait statue with her mom and dad.

I mouth *Amazing* to Devin. She made an entire life-size collage of herself. She found flesh-colored pictures for her skin, and even switched out the green pictures for purple ones to capture her current hair. Pops of plum, orchid, violet, and lavender are arranged into strands and waves. She used pink pictures for a dress, and even put together some collage earrings. The best part is that most of the pictures are actually bits and pieces of her life and personality. She incorporated magazine cut-outs of her favorite K-pop groups, hair dye ads, fried chicken, and kimchi, and a collage of Birkenstock sandals makes up her sculpture's Birkenstock sandals.

Devin flashes me a thumbs-up and I step closer to my model. It looks exactly how I left it, with Jean and Trevor topping pizzas, Denise filing her nails at the delivery station, Jamie washing dishes, Chris and Farrah at the registers, Mom sitting at her desk in the office, and Dad making pizza dough in the prep annex.

At the center of it all is the largest piece of equipment, the oven. Being the person who made it, I recognize my oven, the one that started the day in pieces. Anyone else, however, would just see the sculpted shape of an oven collaged in gray and silver magazine cutouts. On top of the oven, staring me in the face, in magazine cutout lettering, is *Soul Slice 2.0*. My throat tightens. Devin did fix it after all.

"Thank you," I whisper to my friend, and she squeezes my hand.

"They're going to announce the winners," Justin says, pulling my attention to the front of the room.

I watch, wiping my sweaty palms on the skirt of my dress, as one of the judges crosses the stage to hand the announcer the results. I take a deep breath, knowing that inside that envelope is the culmination of everything I've done so far in Hempstead. Winner or not, I gave this festival, the move, and even my delivery job everything that I had to give. And that in itself is a triumph.

"The first-place winner for the design category," the announcer reads, glancing back down at the cue card, "is Maya Reynolds. Judges remarked that not only does it feel like you're in the shop she created, but Maya displayed a clear mastery of various art mediums with her one design."

Did they really say my name? I'm not sure I believe it until I hear Devin screech and wrap me in a hug. I let out a breath, buzzing from shock and joy.

"Congratulations, Maya," the announcer says, before moving on to the next winner.

"Yeah, congrats!" Justin cheers, and before I know it, he's giving me a hug, too. I feel myself blush as he steps away.

Mr. Chris comes over and hands me my first-place ribbon. "Great job, kiddo."

"Thanks, Mr. Chris," I say, beaming at the soft, silky ribbon in my hands. "I couldn't have done it without you, and Devin." I glance from him to Devin and back again.

When Mr. Chris leaves, I gaze at my model of Soul Slice. Every detail stands out to me along with the stories behind them, the stories of how I juggled so many overwhelming changes but still managed to make it to this moment.

Then I hear it—the announcer says Devin's name! She wins first place in the originality category, and when Mr. Chris gives her *her* ribbon, we silently do a little victory dance, flashing our ribbons at each other. As I watch Devin's parents sweep her up in a group hug, I'm hit by a pang of longing. I know my parents are busy doing their thing right now, but my victory feels a little bittersweet without them. I glance at Justin, grateful to have him here.

The announcer taps the mic to get everyone's attention and gives closing remarks. "Don't forget! First-place winners are asked to write a speech and present here on Saturday—the last day of the festival—to our art department donors. This way we can showcase your work and you can tell the people who made this all possible why art is important to you. We look forward to seeing you there, and have a great night!"

I look to Devin, sure that she also forgot to mention *that*, but she and her mom are talking—heads tilted toward each other and Devin gesturing to her project. I don't want to interrupt them, and besides,

I need to get back to Soul Slice. So, Justin and I slip through the crowds and out the door of the gym.

"Congratulations, Maya. You did it!" Justin says as we hurry down the hallway. "Your piece was amazing."

"Thank you," I say, still flushed with joy. But then I feel that pang again, thinking about the speech I'll have to give on Saturday, and my parents.

"I'm sorry about your parents," Justin says, reading my mind.

I sigh. "What's the point in giving a speech when the two people who I care most about hearing it won't even be here?" I ask him.

"Look, after tonight, the Soul Slice opening will be behind them and maybe they'll be able to come," Justin points out.

He's right. That's how it *should* go. But I'm so used to them being unavailable that I'm not even sure anymore.

When I don't say anything, he adds, "And I'll be there."

"You will?" I ask, feeling my face get hot.

"Yeah, wouldn't want to miss it."

My phone vibrates with the *All good?* text from Mom. This time, I reply—not wanting to raise any suspicion. I tell her that I'm on my way back now.

We reach the spot in the hallway where we stashed the pizza box and the bag with my uniform. They—and the trash can they were behind—are all gone.

My heart stops.

"The janitor must have come by," Justin reasons.

"Crap, what am I going to do? I can't go back to work looking like this!" I gesture down to my dress. It'll be a dead giveaway.

We split up. Justin jogs down the hallway and looks for any other trash cans and checks behind the water fountains, but there's no sign of my bag. I duck into the girls' bathroom to double-check that my stuff didn't end up in there. No luck.

With no extra time to spare, we leave school and start walking, Justin pushing my bike along for me. We try to come up with a scheme, some way for me to spin this to avoid getting in trouble. But by the time we roll to a stop in front of Soul Slice—still bumpin' with customers, and now music—we have no concrete plan.

"Maya," someone hisses when I get behind the counter.

Denise looks over her shoulder toward the office before coming the rest of the way into the delivery station.

"Girl, your parents are looking for you," she says, doing a double take to soak in my change of clothes. "Look at you!"

I blush, feeling somewhat exposed in a dress instead of my uniform. Speaking of which . . .

"Denise, I lost my uniform at school."

"I'm sure there are some extras in the office," she says, then glances at Justin. He gives both of us a small wave before turning to greet his dad in the crowd.

"I'll try to find a shirt that I can put over this," I say, shifting past Denise toward the back of the shop.

"Why? Don't you want to stay cute for your date?" she asks.

"Denise, it wasn't a date. It was a *festival*," I correct her, embarrassed.

"What festival? Maya, what are you doing in that dress?" Mom asks, coming up behind me. "What's going on?"

I'm caught. I have no idea how to answer.

"Office, *now*," Mom says, the *tone* coming out.

Denise mouths *Sorry* to me before I turn around and follow Mom. I glance back at Justin, but he's talking to his dad and some other folks.

Mom motions to Dad, who's helping Jean on the topping line, to come with us. When he sees me in the dress, confusion passes over his face, and he immediately takes off his apron and files into the office.

"What's wrong?" he asks, gently closing the door.

"I don't know. She's about to tell us," Mom says, her tone accusatory. "I heard her talking with Denise about going on a date to a festival."

"The art festival?" Dad asks, looking at me.

I could lie. I could make something up and say I wanted to wear my dress for the opening and figured since they didn't want me taking deliveries that it wouldn't hurt to change out of my uniform. I could try to make myself sound cute and innocent by telling them that I wanted to surprise them by matching the shop, and I used a delivery as an excuse to change, and—

"I went to the art festival at school," I say. No matter

my punishment, no matter how upset my parents get, I know that I wouldn't change any one moment from the past few weeks. And if I believe in every decision I made, then I don't want to pretend that none of it happened.

"*Maya*, we said *no*. What were you thinking?" Mom asks, eyes wide.

"I was thinking that I wanted to fit in at my new school, where I had to make all new friends even though I didn't have time to hang out with them. I wasn't even allowed to have time to settle in—we moved here and I had to start working." I pause to take a breath. "I've spent the past few weeks putting together my best art project. You've been working toward the grand opening all this time, and even though I've been here, *I've* been working toward the festival. I'm sorry . . . but that's the truth."

I pull out my ribbon, running my fingers over the soft fabric and holding on to what Mom said to me about wanting me to do more, to follow my passions. Mom and Dad say nothing, just look at me with surprised expressions.

"I know I wasn't as enthusiastic about the move as I could've been, but I supported you," I go on. "My first day making deliveries, I didn't fall off my bike. I tripped in front of a customer and fell face-first into their pizza. I was embarrassed, too embarrassed to tell you because I didn't want to disappoint you.

"And instead of trying to get out of having to do any more deliveries, I gave it a chance. I kept an open mind because I knew you needed me to. *You* needed me to show up, to be efficient, and I did all of that. The festival is what *I* needed."

I hand Mom the ribbon with the little card pinned to the back. It's an invitation to the speech ceremony on Saturday.

"Soul Slice is your dream, but art and design are mine. Just like you guys, my hard work paid off. I figured you would be proud, if you could've been there. I know that you've been putting so much into the shop, but we made it to this day. We could've left for a little while together, and you could've—"

I sob, tears streaming down my face and my nose running—all gross and stuff. But I can't help it. I remember how it felt to be standing there next to all my hard work and realizing that, without my parents, I didn't care who saw it or how great any judge thought it was.

"I just wish you could've been there."

Before either of them can speak, I use the back of my hands to wipe my face and mumble that I'm going to finish my shift, and that I'm sorry I disobeyed them and I know I'll probably be grounded or something.

I'm thankful that they don't stop me on my way out.

chapter 18

Later that night, after I'm showered and my hair is wrapped up and my dress is hanging on my closet door, I lie on my bed and stare at the ceiling. I know my reckoning is coming, and I already texted Sasha to warn her that she might not hear from me if my phone gets taken away. Still, though, I can't deny that tonight was pretty good. I truly am happy for my parents. The Soul Slice opening was a hit, and we made more money tonight than we had on any given day at the Brooklyn Soul Slice. If that's not a good sign, I don't know what is.

And even without my parents there, winning the art show was awesome. Devin is a great friend, and I can't wait to have the chance to come through for her the way she has for me. I've decided I'll start by teaching her how to make Fried Chicken and Waffle pizza for herself. It was her request, in case she ever gets a craving when the shop is closed or something.

Then there's Justin. Saying he'll come see my speech . . . Saying he's not friends with Waverly. I really need to know what that's about.

"Maya."

I look over to see Mom and Dad filling my doorway. They come in, and I sit up, making room for them to sit on either side of me.

"I think this belongs to you," Mom says, handing me my ribbon.

I take it quietly, scared of what's coming next. I'm grounded for a week—two weeks? No phone, no Sasha. No art supplies, or no art *club* for the rest of the semester?

"We're sorry," Dad says.

I look up from the ribbon in my hands to see his face, sure I misheard him.

"You're right," he goes on. "As owners of Soul Slice, it was on us to hire workers. You should've never been in a position to have to do what you did," he tells me, giving me a slight nudge with his shoulder.

"But you did *do* it; you showed up every day, and you worked your butt off and did your part to make *our* dream come true," Mom says. "You supported us and we should've tried harder to support you, and for that we are sorry, honey."

"Sometimes we forget that you're our little girl. You're our daughter, but you act so self-sufficient and independent—and we *admire* that, but I think somewhere along the way with this move we lost sight of our responsibility," Dad says.

"*You* are our dream. Our first dream. Our biggest dream. The most important dream, Maya," Mom says, wrapping her arm around my shoulder. "We joke sometimes that the shop is our first child, but you are our *only* baby. You're the one we held in our arms and brought home from the hospital; you're the one we stayed up with at night—fed, diapered, and rocked. You will always be more important to us than the shop, and we just want to make sure you know that."

"I do know that," I say, trying not to get teary-eyed.

"And I don't want you guys to think that I didn't want to help out, because I did. I was just caught off guard when it turned out to be a full-time thing." Remembering what Justin said about talking to my parents, being honest about how I feel, I add, "I just didn't think it was fair when it cut into my art, and when it cut into me being a kid and making friends and trying to put my new life together."

"We know," Dad says, his tone saturated with apology. "We know that the move has been hard and stressful—we guessed that it would be way back when we heard you telling Sasha that it wasn't happening, that it was some kind of prank." He and Mom laugh at the memory, and I can't help but smile at how ridiculous that must have sounded.

"We should've talked to you more, and checked in," Mom says. "Even though we can't change the way these past few weeks have been, we promise that we are going to do better."

"Starting with this ceremony," Dad says, slipping the ribbon out of my hand. He opens the card, pretending to read it, and says, "Our daughter's art is *so* good that they want her to give a speech to the whooooole country about why art is important."

"It's not the whole country," I say, laughing at his imitation of an English accent.

"The whooooole school," he revises.

"More like the whooooole auditorium of people that decide to come," I say, smiling.

"Which will include us," Mom assures me.

"I want you to be there," I tell them, "but I know Saturday is one of the busiest nights at the shop. I'd understand if you can't come. I'm just happy that you guys finally see what my art means to me."

"We really do," Mom says, her voice cracking a little. She and Dad lean in, squishing me with a group hug that I couldn't be happier to be part of.

I try to reach my arms around them to hug them, too, finally feeling like we all are really in this together. It reminds me of that night at the seafood restaurant when I tried crayfish. We were in a new place with no idea what to do, and we took a risk—just the three of us.

"We'll be there. You can count on it," Dad assures me when we pull apart.

"I mean, we didn't hire all these people so that they wouldn't have to work," Mom reasons.

"I love you guys," I say, knowing that I haven't said it nearly enough.

"We love you, too."

"And look, it's not like we'll never go back to Brooklyn," Dad adds.

"Yeah, we have to check on the shop," Mom chimes in.

"Make sure Thomas isn't eating *all* the cheese," Dad adds, making us laugh.

"Plus, we want you to still see Sasha. Maybe for holidays or weekend sleepovers," Mom says.

"That would be awesome," I say, feeling warm and excited at the prospect. "Maybe Sasha could even come here sometime." She could see the new Soul Slice, meet Devin . . . and meet Justin, too.

o♥o♥o

On Saturday, I'm a bundle of nerves, pacing outside the entrance to the gym. Mom and Dad are already inside, having picked front-row seats to the stage that was set up for the speech ceremony. And Devin is backstage, feeling confident since we spent hours yesterday rehearsing our speeches in front of each other.

The speech isn't what I'm worried about.

I check my phone, seeing that it's been ten minutes since Justin said he would meet me in ten minutes! Open communication helped me with my parents, so hopefully it will help me finally make things right with Justin.

He rounds the corner at the end of the hall and jogs the rest of the way to me, only huffing and puffing a little bit.

"Seriously, I think you're selling yourself short with baseball," I tease.

Justin laughs in between catching his breath. "So, you got jokes, Miss *First Place*."

"Maybe just a few," I say, trying not to lose my nerve.

"What's up? Everything okay?" he asks.

"No—I mean, yes. Everything is okay. I just wanted to say that you were right about talking to my parents. We had a heart-to-heart after the grand opening, and I feel like I can finally relax now and *be* here—in Hempstead, you know?"

"You reached your equilibrium," he says, smiling so that his dimple peeks out.

I say, "Yes, I guess I did."

"That's great, Maya."

"It's not the only thing I wanted to talk about," I admit, fidgeting with the corner of my speech cards. "Um, I'm really glad that we met and you helped make moving to a new place less intimidating and more . . . entertaining."

"Entertaining?" he asks, amused.

"When I would vent to my best friend from back home about everything that was happening, she used to say my life here was like a sitcom, and most of that came from you," I say, feeling a little embarrassed but also happy to share that with him. "You made it colorful."

He just looks at me, his honey-brown eyes searching for something—my point, probably.

"I think you're really great, and nice, and easy to talk to. And you're good at making pizza, and I'm sure you're great at cooking other things, too," I start rambling, pulling myself back when the next natural compliment that materializes in my head is about how once again he's cleaned up really nice. The khakis aren't so bad when he pairs them with colorful print button-downs.

"I think you're great, too, Maya," he says, pulling me from the spiral of thoughts twisting in my head. "Now that I'm an *expert* pizza maker," he adds, laughing because we both know that's not entirely true, "we'll have to find something else to do together."

I feel my face get hot at the suggestion.

Justin is more than great. He's cute, funny, *smart*—I mean, *homeostasis*? Come on!—and easy to talk to. What Sasha said, about how I'll never know anything about him if I don't ask, comes to mind.

The moment that really got me thinking was when David and Carter got all weird at the grand opening. I tell Justin about it, asking, "What did you tell them?"

His face catches red undertones, exposing that he has something to hide.

"Come on, out with it," I say when he doesn't offer an answer.

"I may have told them that you have a boyfriend," he admits, looking at the ground.

"But I *don't* have a boyfriend," I point out.

"Well, maybe you do—or, I mean, you could if you wanted to . . ."

"I could?" I lead him with my tone, waiting for him to look at me.

All you have to do is tell the truth.

Shooting my shot, I say, "Because I'd want one . . ."

This makes him look up, his eyes bright. I realize how cute his smile is. He has the slight snaggle tooth, a dimple, and on top of that, his smile is familiar and comforting. It's the smile that makes Hempstead feel like home to me.

"I like you, Justin Baker."

"I like you a lot, Maya Reynolds," he says.

No doubts or reservations, with everything laid out, I lean up on my toes and press my lips against his. Justin leans in, too, wrapping his arms around my waist. I reach up and run my hand over his barber fade and waves, feeling the ripples under my fingertips. He's all mine, sweeter than the syrup on a Fried Chicken and Waffle slice.

My first kiss! With Justin!

"Maya," someone hisses.

We snap apart, and I turn around to see Devin leaning out of the auditorium's backstage doors, shaking her head with a smile on her face.

"Glad to see you guys *made up*," she teases. "Now, come on. It's showtime."

I turn back to Justin, feeling a little sad that he has to sit in the audience instead of hang out backstage with us—

"His lips will be there when you're done," Devin groans sarcastically.

"Oh. My. Gosh!" I squeal, embarrassed but undoubtedly happy.

"Good luck," Justin says, squeezing my hand and taking a step back toward the audience entrance. "I mean, not that you'll need it."

"Thanks," I say.

Before I can add anything else, Devin grabs my

arm and pulls me into the backstage darkness. When the door latches closed, I begin to come out from under the spell of the kiss. I rearrange my speech cards and fall in line with the other winners, waiting for my name to be called.

When it's my turn to give my speech, I take the stage and look out at the audience. I see Justin sitting with Devin's parents. In the front row, Mom and Dad smile up at me, Mom waving and Dad holding up his phone to take a video. Mr. Chris is standing to the side with some of the other teachers.

When Dad snaps a photo, illuminating himself with the flash, it makes me happy, knowing that we'll be able to hold on to today forever.

The speech . . . my first kiss . . .

I take a deep breath to steady myself, feeling heat rise in my cheeks. I glance down at my cue cards, and begin.

"My piece is the model of the Soul Slice pizza shop. My inspiration came from my amazing, hardworking, and loving parents."

I look out at the audience. Dad snaps another

picture, and Mom reaches for his arm to get him to stop. Behind them, I lock eyes with Justin. He smiles at me, a smile that feels bigger than the past month. It makes me smile, too.

"And," I continue, "all the elements that I put into my project, that made it unique and special enough to win this award, came together with the help of my new friends and some great pizza . . ."

Acknowledgments

First, I want to thank Aimee Friedman for being a great editor and a joy to work with. Without you (and your patience with me!), this project wouldn't have been possible. I'm so glad that I had the opportunity to work with you and hope we can do it again soon.

Next, I'd like to thank my agent, John Cusick. This adventure is only just beginning and you continue to spearhead my dreams like no other.

A big thanks to Taylor McManus and Yaffa Jaskoll for illustrating and designing a cover that captures Maya's vibrant personality. I'm still so impressed by it and can't wait for readers to fall for it as hard as I did!

Thank you to everyone at Scholastic who came together to make *Pizza My Heart* what it is.

Finally, I'd like to thank the friends who let me talk in circles as I pieced the story together, and my best friend and my family for always supporting and encouraging me as I pursue my dream.

In the same way that Maya was uprooted from the world she knew and dropped into an unfamiliar town, my move to Ohio three years ago was sudden and equally (if not more, lol) turbulent. It turned out to be one of the best decisions I've made, and the friends who came together and welcomed me are the reason I was able to flourish and succeed. So, thank you to Brittany, Sam, Sky, Nicole, Bailey, and Colleen. I guess you could say you all have a pizza my heart . . . Oh, I went there!

Have you read all the (wish) books?

- [ ] *Twice Upon a Time: Sleeping Beauty, the One Who Took the Really Long Nap* by Wendy Mass
- [ ] *True to Your Selfie* by Megan McCafferty
- [ ] *Blizzard Besties* by Yamile Saied Méndez
- [ ] *Random Acts of Kittens* by Yamile Saied Méndez
- [ ] *Wish Upon a Stray* by Yamile Saied Méndez
- [ ] *Playing Cupid* by Jenny Meyerhoff
- [ ] *Cake Pop Crush* by Suzanne Nelson
- [ ] *Macarons at Midnight* by Suzanne Nelson
- [ ] *Hot Cocoa Hearts* by Suzanne Nelson
- [ ] *You're Bacon Me Crazy* by Suzanne Nelson
- [ ] *Donut Go Breaking My Heart* by Suzanne Nelson
- [ ] *Sundae My Prince Will Come* by Suzanne Nelson
- [ ] *I Only Have Pies for You* by Suzanne Nelson
- [ ] *Shake It Off* by Suzanne Nelson
- [ ] *Pumpkin Spice Up Your Life* by Suzanne Nelson
- [ ] *A Batch Made in Heaven* by Suzanne Nelson
- [ ] *Confectionately Yours: Save the Cupcake!* by Lisa Papademetriou
- [ ] *Pizza My Heart* by Rhiannon Richardson
- [ ] *My Secret Guide to Paris* by Lisa Schroeder
- [ ] *Sealed with a Secret* by Lisa Schroeder
- [ ] *Switched at Birthday* by Natalie Standiford
- [ ] *The Only Girl in School* by Natalie Standiford
- [ ] *Clique Here* by Anna Staniszewski
- [ ] *Double Clique* by Anna Staniszewski
- [ ] *Once Upon a Cruise* by Anna Staniszewski
- [ ] *Deep Down Popular* by Phoebe Stone
- [ ] *Meow or Never* by Jazz Taylor
- [ ] *Revenge of the Flower Girls* by Jennifer Ziegler
- [ ] *Revenge of the Angels* by Jennifer Ziegler

Read the latest *wish* books!